Valerie Bloom was born in Cl... came to England in 1979. ... African and Caribbean literat... University of Kent and was a... Masters degree from the university in 1995.

Valerie has conducted lots of writing and perform-ance workshops in shools and colleges and has per-formed ... ... Caribbean. Her poems have been ... ... the National Curriculum and have appeared in *Poems on the Underground* and as the *Independent* newspaper's Poem of the Day.

One River, Many Creeks, poems from all around the world is also published by Macmillan.

Surprising Joy is Valerie's first novel.

*This is Valerie Bloom's first novel but she
has published many wonderful collections
of poetry as well. These include:*

Fruits
Ackee, Breadfruit, Callaloo
One River, Many Creeks
Whoop an' Shout!

Valerie Bloom

MACMILLAN CHILDREN'S BOOKS

First published 2003 by Macmillan's Children's Books

This edition published 2004 by Macmillan Children's Books
a division of Macmillan Publishers Limited
20 New Wharf Road, London N1 9RR
Basingstoke and Oxford
www.panmacmillan.com

Associated companies throughout the world

ISBN 0 330 39860 1

A CIP catalogue record for this book is available from
the British Library.

Phototypeset by Intype Libra Ltd
Printed and bound in Great Britain by Mackays of Chatham plc, Kent

For Douglas, Tamara, Ashley and Jody with love

*With special thanks to Polly Nolan for all her hard
work, and especially her patience*

Part One:

JAMAICA

Chapter One

D'you know what my problem is? My mouth doesn't know when to stay shut, and one of these days I just know it's going to get me into serious trouble. It's not that I talk too much, although I know some people might argue with that. If that was the trouble I could probably force myself to keep quiet sometimes. The problem is that every now and then I blurt out what I'm thinking without meaning to. You know, sometimes you might be saying one thing and thinking something else entirely that you don't want the person you're with to know about particularly? Well sometimes my brain doesn't know the difference and it will engage my mouth when it should be putting on the brake.

Take that day at the post office for instance. I didn't really expect a letter that day. I'd just posted mine to Mama the week before and it was too early for her to reply, but out of habit I went with Nadine up the road to the post office. I sometimes wished that we lived in Kingston where the mail was delivered to the door. Out in the country, we had to queue at a window in the post office and wait while the postmistress checked to see if we'd got any letters.

1

'Any letters for Lilith or Joy Patterson, please?' I recited the words as usual but, as I said, I wasn't expecting anything, so I was watching Nadine at the window next to me. She was playing cat's cradle with a piece of string she'd fished out of her uniform pocket while her letter box was checked by the other postmistress.

Most times she only took two seconds to look through the letters in the 'P' cubbyhole before she said 'no, nothing', so it was only when she said, 'Here it is,' that I realized that she was holding an airmail letter through the window to me. It was registered and I signed for it, with my heart galloping like a runaway donkey.

A registered letter usually meant money from abroad, either for me or for Granny. If it was from America that meant the money was Gran's, but if it was from England I had a fifty–fifty chance of getting some cash. And who could tell. It might be the letter I'd been waiting for.

I shut my eyes and sent up a little prayer before I looked at the postmark. Yes! It was from England. I turned it over as I was walking to the steps of the post office. My heart slowed as disappointment swallowed all the excitement. It wasn't from Mama.

'Just because you get letter, you too good to walk with me now?'

I was so wrapped up in the letter I completely forgot to wait for Nadine. I stuffed it into my school bag and hooked my arm through hers to show I wasn't vexed with her or anything, even though I knew she was just joking.

'Sorry,' I said. 'I forget. I was thinking Mama write me, but is only from Cousin Sophie for Granny. You get any?'

'Not a message.' She gave me a sideways look. 'So you not going to England then?'

'What you talking 'bout?'

'Well you always saying how you just waiting for a letter from you mother and you gone to England.'

'Lord give me strength, Nadine, what wrong with you? How much time I have to tell you. Me mother sending for me next year.' Boy, you can be so stupid sometimes, I thought. 'Course, I didn't mean to say that aloud, but my stupid mouth just blurt it out.

'Who you calling stupid? You think because you going to England you better than anybody?'

I opened my mouth to say something spiteful and then I saw her face. I linked my hand in hers. 'I sorry, Nadine. I didn't mean it you know.'

She looked at me and a little smile brightened her face. 'A'right . . . Race you down the road.'

We were on a little hill above the main road and there was a lane with iron railings along the side. People were supposed to use the lane to get to and from the post office, but all the school children ducked underneath the railings so that now there was a little spider web of shortcuts in the red earth from the lane to the main road.

Nadine was almost under the railings before I

realized what she was doing. I dashed after her but she scooted underneath and, because I was so tall, it took me longer to get under. I was tearing after her shouting, 'Wait, Nadine. Me wasn't ready yet!' She was speeding across the road, her two pigtails flying out behind her.

I was focusing on the pigtails, trying to shorten the distance between us. With my long legs you would think I could catch her easily, but Nadine was like a rabbit when she got going. I was concentrating so hard on catching up that I didn't see Maas Josh and his handcart.

Maas Josh was the smallest man I'd ever seen. He couldn't have been more than about four and a half feet tall. I borrowed a book of fairy tales from the library once and there was a gnome in it, the spitting image of Maas Josh. It had the same squashed face that looked like maybe a mule had sat on it by mistake, the same tiny eyes and the same feet that looked too big for his body and turned out like they were not on speaking terms with each other.

Maas Josh used his handcart to wheel his ice-cream bucket 'round town every day. On our way to school we would see him churning the ice cream under the big guangu tree in front of the market. By recess time the ice cream was ready, pink and melt-in-your-mouth delicious and we'd troop out to the school gate with our dollars, where he'd be waiting. It was much better ice cream than you could get in the shops.

That day being Friday, he must have been selling in the market and was pushing the empty ice-cream bucket home. Nadine scooted across the road in front of him, and I, just behind her, was unable to stop myself and ran slap into the handcart. The air rushed from my lungs like a burst balloon. I was flat on my back in the middle of the road, spread out like a squashed bull frog.

There wasn't very much excitement in Prospect at the best of times. I remember once everybody came out when a bull broke its rope and galloped through the village. So before I had a chance to get up and recover myself, a crowd had gathered round me. The embarrassment was killing me, the sun was blinding me and I closed my eyes. That was a mistake.

'Who-ooh! Maas Josh, you kill Sister Patterson one grand pickney!'

'She dead? Who dead?'

'Is Joy. Sister Patterson little girl.'

'Give the pickney air. You all don't crowd round her so.'

'She don't have no use for air if she dead. Pickney, you dead?'

And poor Maas Josh was trying to tell anyone who would listen, 'Is not my fault. She just come flyin' down the bank into the middle o' the road.'

Someone agreed with him. 'Yes I did see it, Maas Josh. I will be a witness if you need one.'

'Thank you, Ma'am. Dem chil'ren would o' never

look where dem going. Suppose was a car coming instead of me handcart? She would o' dead for true.'

'You think we should move her?' someone else asked. Well is about time, I thought. I could be really dead for all they know and they standing there arguing over how to share out the blame.

'No, you not suppose to move a accident victim. You might interfere with the broke bones.'

'Who say she have any broke bone?'

'Maas Josh, I hope you handcart insure, for this bound to cost you.'

'Somebody get a car. We going have to take her to the hospital.'

My eyes flew open then. I couldn't lie there and allow them to cart me off to hospital.

'Praise the Lord, she not dead. Pickney, how you feeling? Which part it hurt?'

I got up, brushed the dust off my uniform and picked up my bag. Now that I'd recovered my breath, the thing hurting most was my pride. I hardly noticed the twinge in my side where I'd connected with the handcart. Nadine's frightened face was peering at me.

'I all right,' I said. 'I not hurting anywhere.'

Maas Josh took off his battered felt hat, wiped his forehead with the back of his hand and jammed the hat back on his head. He looked more like a gnome than ever.

'You not hurting anywhere?' he asked. 'You sure?'

I nodded. I think he saw that as adding insult to injury.

'So what you mean by jumping in front me hand-cart like that? You trying to give me heart attack or what? When I see you there on the ground I say to meself, "Lord, I kill the chile." An' you stand up there telling me you not hurting. I have a good mind to . . .'

'Control youself, Maas Joshie! No harm no done. Make the child go on home to her grandmother. Come on, chile, run home to you granny you hear.'

I turned gratefully to the woman who had come over from her shop across the road.

'Yes, ma'am,' I said and turned to leave. The crowd was walking away, disappointed that there wasn't going to be an ambulance or a police car in the district today.

'And next time look before you gallop into the road, you hear. I going to talk to you granny 'bout you. Some o' you shouldn't let out on the street. You all too dangerous.'

I made up my mind not to buy any more ice cream from Maas Josh.

Nadine came and linked her hand through mine and we walked off. Neither of us said anything until we were out of sight of the few people still standing around Maas Josh. Then Nadine was the first to speak.

'Boy, Joy, you frighten me. I think you dead for true.'

'Nadine, how much people you hear handcart kill?' I asked scornfully.

7

'But, Joy man, you did look dead with you eye dem shut like that.'

'Well, as you see, me no dead.' I was getting tired of the conversation. I didn't want to remember how stupid I'd been. Since infant school they'd been drumming it into us: 'Look before you cross the road'. It's true that in Prospect you didn't usually have very much to look for. Not too many people had cars, and since the district wasn't a short cut to anywhere, not too many vehicles passed through either.

But that was no excuse. I could just imagine how Granny would carry on when Maas Josh told her. It didn't bear thinking about.

'And it would o' be my fault.' Nadine was like a dog with a bone when she got hold of an idea.

'Nadine, don't talk stupid. Me should o' look where me was going. Now just forget it, OK?'

Nadine nodded. 'You want to go and pick abbe?'

The abbe were like tiny coconuts, the size of cherries. We had to break them open with flint stones. If we were lucky, the hard shell would crack open and the nut would come out whole, but most times it would splinter into little pieces and we had to pick them up bit by bit off the dried leaves on the ground.

'No, I have to get home.'

We walked in silence for a while. Nadine tried to make conversation, but even she soon got tired of one-word answers.

'Why you so quiet today?' Nadine peered into my face. 'You fretting 'bout what you gran going to say when she hear 'bout the accident?'

'Cho, I not thinking 'bout that. I have better things to worry 'bout.'

But I didn't look at her, and we were both quiet after that. To be honest, I wasn't thinking of anything else. Granny was very poorly and I didn't know what news like that could do to her blood pressure. I had to think of some way to prevent Maas Josh from telling Gran about the accident.

'You stopping?' Nadine asked when we got to the track leading up to her house. I sometimes stopped to play with her on my way home. To tell you the truth, it was more for Nadine's mum's sweet potato pudding, which was always waiting for us and tasted like something the angels would leave heaven to have, but I didn't feel very sociable today.

'No thanks, I have to go and see how Granny is. She wasn't feeling too well when I left this morning.'

'Is her blood pressure again?'

'Mmm.'

'See you Monday then.'

'All right, see you Monday.'

Nadine quickly flung out her hand and hit me on the arm before I could get away.

'Last lick!' she shouted as she ran up the track.

Usually, if she managed to get her touch in before me, I would chase her and try to get the last touch for the day because I hate to lose. But today winning didn't seem so important. So I just shouted after her, 'I will catch you Monday!'

I watched until her blue uniform disappeared round the bend in the track. Then I turned and went back the way we had come. I had to talk to Maas Josh before I went home.

Chapter Two

I headed back towards the post office. I was rehearsing what I was going to say to Maas Josh to try to persuade him not to come and complain to Gran.

I could tell him that Gran had gone to Kingston for a few days and wouldn't be back till the weekend. I could tell him that Gran had a bad heart and any disagreeable news could kill her. But that was silly. I was a terrible liar anyway. I blame it on Gran and her church. She's always drumming Christian virtues into me, so that now I find it hard to sin with a clear conscience.

I decided just to tell him the truth and appeal to his good judgement not to disturb Granny now. People in Prospect didn't like to hear of their children causing problems. They thought it reflected badly on them and that other people would think they were failing in their duty. It was bad enough when another child complained about you, but when an adult did, it was serious. The shame was not just yours, but your parents' as well. Gran didn't need this just now.

As soon as I reached the bend before the town, I saw Maas Josh pushing his handcart up the road. It was like a good sign to me. I didn't relish the idea of talking to him in the town where somebody else was bound to overhear.

'Excuse me, Maas Josh,' I said, with what I thought was deepest humility.

Maas Josh stopped the handcart and came round to stand protectively beside it as if he thought I was going to run at it and knock myself over again.

'What you want?' he asked suspiciously.

'I sorry I bump into you handcart, sir.'

He wasn't sure how to take this. He stared at me a minute longer, then said gruffly, 'Well look where you going next time and don't do it again. If it was a car you would dead by now, you know.'

'Yes, sir.'

We stood like that eyeing each other warily, me wondering how to ask the question on my mind, he probably wondering what I was going to get up to next.

'Well,' he moved back between the shafts of his handcart and prepared to continue on his way. 'Don't do it again.'

'I can ask you a favour, please, sir?'

'Favour? What kind o' favour?' He was immediately suspicious again. I sighed. It is a hard thing not to be trusted.

'Well, is me gran, sir. She not too well and I 'fraid if you tell her 'bout the little accident now, it might make her worse.'

'I see.' He said it like he saw a lot more than there

was to see. He thought I was just trying to save my own skin. I had to make him see it could harm Gran to have anything else to worry about.

'I don't mind if you tell her when she get better, Maas Josh,' I said. 'But her blood pressure really high and it will get higher if you tell her now.'

'A soh?'

I nodded vigorously.

He tilted his head to one side, like a little bird considering a worm.

'She really bad, you know, Maas Josh, and if you tell her, that will send her blood pressure up higher and she might get so sick that they might have to take her into hospital, and then they would come and take me because pickney not suppose to live on they own, and when Granny come back and find out that me not there, she will get upset and get sick again and have to go back into hospital and she might even dead and I know you wouldn't want that on you conscience.'

'A'right. A'right.' Maas Josh threw up his hands in surrender. He was looking at me as if I was from another planet. 'You better go home to Sister Patterson now,' he said. 'If she so sick, she bound to need you.'

'Yes, sir. Thank you, sir.'

I was almost skipping on my way home.

Chapter Three

Granny was still in bed. I threw my school bag on to my bed and tiptoed into her room. I could see she was worse than when I left for school. Her mouth was drawn up into a tight pouch with pain and her forehead glistened with moisture like young banana leaves in the early morning dew. I crept over to kneel by her bedside. I knew she had to be bad to have stayed in bed all day.

'Evening, Granny.'

I don't know why I was whispering, except that her eyes were closed. But from her uneven breathing and the occasional grunt of pain I knew that she wasn't asleep. Her eyes fluttered open and she turned her head towards me, slowly, as if she was afraid it would fall off if she moved it any faster.

'You come, me pickney?' She was whispering as well, but only because she was too ill to speak any louder. 'Beg you go out the back and pick some . . . some . . .' Her hand moved feebly trying to grasp the word that was just out of reach. Her memory was getting worse too, but I knew what she wanted.

Out in the backyard, I collected what I needed.

Some periwinkle leaves, a couple of flowers from the passion-fruit vine that was climbing all over the Milly mango tree, and a few of the softest leaves near the top of the little Queen of the Meadow bush. The soursop leaves were more difficult. I wanted a couple of big ones but the lowest branch was way over my head. I had to wrap my legs round the trunk and pull myself up until I could hold on to the branch and swing my legs up and over.

If Granny could see me now she would probably have a heart attack on top of all her other worries. She was always saying it was time for me to stop behaving like a tomboy and act like the young lady I was. She had no idea how much fun you could get from climbing trees.

My uniform was tree-bark stained when I came down. I knew I should have changed before I tackled the soursop tree but this was an emergency. All the same, after I'd put the passion flowers, Queen of the Meadow leaves and the periwinkle in a pan to boil with some crushed garlic, I went to change into my yard clothes. I didn't want to upset Granny. I would wash out the uniform after I finished cooking the dinner.

The water was boiling away when I got back into the kitchen. I poured some into a mug, added some sugar and took it in to Gran with the soursop leaves. There was a bottle of bay rum on the table beside her bed. I placed the mug and the leaves on the table and went to lay my hand against Gran's forehead. It was burning. I loosened her head-tie and her thick white hair fell free. I felt a cloud of fear settle over my head because I knew now that Granny was really sick. She would never leave her hair unplaited all day unless she was very bad.

I took the bay rum, poured a little into my hand and rubbed it over her head, face and forehead. She moaned softly and I stopped, scared that I was hurting her, but she opened her eyes and a tired half-smile lifted the corners of her mouth, ironing out the lines mapping her face.

'Just a little more, me love,' she said.

'OK, Granny.' I poured some more bay rum into my hand. 'But make sure you tell me if it hurt.'

Another tilt of the mouth corners, but she just grunted.

I put the soursop leaves on her forehead and re-tied her head-tie over them. I didn't know how they worked, but they always made her feel better. I handed her the mug of tea.

'Thank you, me child. God bless you,' she whispered.

I felt my throat tighten and the back of my eyes start to sting. Granny's attacks were becoming more and more frequent and each time they seemed to get worse. I think I would die if anything happened to her. I couldn't remember much about Papa's death. I was just over three when the wall he was building collapsed on him, and even Grandpa's death a year later didn't leave too much of a scar.

Granny herself seemed to soften when Grandpa went, and now, although I dreamed day and night about being with Mama in England, Granny was a second mother to me. I thought how upset she'd have been if Maas Josh had done what he'd threatened to do and come to tell on me. Thank goodness I'd stopped him.

I went to the kitchen to cook the dinner. I had to try and find something to cook that Gran could eat. There was a huge pumpkin and some yams in the basket by the kitchen door. I noticed them as soon as I went in and I grinned to myself. No problem. Gran could never resist pumpkin soup.

I was peeling a slice of the pumpkin when I heard him.

'Mind you dog!'

My heart jumped like a startled bullfrog. Maas Josh! I couldn't believe he would do this to me. He had promised. More or less. But now he was here, and Gran too weak to cope with what he had to say. You just couldn't trust some people. What was I going to do now? Stupid idiot. I was sure he'd meant he wouldn't say anything. But now I thought about it, he hadn't actually said he wouldn't tell. He'd just let me believe he wouldn't. And now here he was on the veranda.

'Anybody dey home?'

I decided I had to go and talk to him. Perhaps I could persuade him that Granny was too sick to see anyone. That was the truth, in my opinion anyway.

'Oh, I was just thinking nobody dey home.' I watched him lower the sack and the machete he was carrying on to the veranda. I had a good mind to run and push him back down the steps before he could do his damage.

'I come to see you granny. How she is?' Did he have to shout?

'She sick bad, Maas Josh.'

'A soh?' He looked hard at me for a minute.

'Yes, sir. I don't think she can see anybody now for she sleeping. Maybe you could come back tomorrow?'

He bent to pick up his sack. 'I sorry to hear that. I bring . . .'

'Joy, who that out there with you?'

Thanks, Gran. Perfect timing. Just when it looked like I was about to persuade Maas Josh to come back some other time. The only good thing was that her voice was so feeble he was bound to realize I'd not been exaggerating.

'Excuse me, Maas Josh.' I turned to go to Gran's room. 'I think we must o' wake her up.' I hoped he got the message that he was to blame.

Granny had propped herself up on the pillows. It must have taken some effort because she was still panting a little

'Granny, you all right?'

She waved away my concern. 'Who you talking to outside?'

'Is Maas Josh, ma'am.'

'Maas Joshie? Him gawn?'

'No, ma'am, him still on the veranda.'

'You left the big man on the veranda? You don't offer him a seat and some refreshment? Girl, where you manners? Go and invite the man inside.'

I went back to the veranda with my tail between my legs. Maas Josh was standing where I left him, turning his felt hat over and over in his hand.

'Granny say for you to come inside please, Maas Josh.'

He followed me into Gran's room, clutching his felt hat close to his chest. I thought he was going to bow when he saw her.

'Sister Patterson,' he said. 'I hear you wasn't feeling too well, so I say let me come and see if I can do anything to help.'

'Thank you, Maas Joshie. Me glad to see you. Sorry I can't get up.' She saw me hovering. I was waiting in dread for Maas Josh to tell her about the accident and thinking maybe I should find the smelling salts just in case. And I forgot my manners again.

'Joy, get Maas Joshie a seat make him take the weight off him foot them. Lord, give me strength. What's the matter with you today, girl?' She turned back to him. 'What I can offer you to drink Maas Joshie?'

I came back with the chair and the glass of water he'd asked for to find them discussing Maas Josh's family. I glanced quickly at Gran, but she didn't look too concerned. In fact, the company seemed to be doing her good because she looked a bit better. So he couldn't have told her yet.

I wanted to be there when Gran learned about the accident, but I knew better than to hang around when big people were talking. I went back to the kitchen and the pumpkin soup with my heart heavy as a river rock stone in my chest.

While I peeled and cut up pumpkins, yams, cho-cho and carrots, I was waiting to be called in to explain my behaviour on the street. I heard Maas Josh leaving Gran's room and going towards the veranda. He was leaving without saying goodbye to me. That was not a good sign. I waited with my heart in my mouth for Granny's call, which is probably why I didn't hear Maas Josh come into the kitchen and I jumped when he spoke just behind me.

'You have a mug I can put this in for you granny, Joy?'

He held out a green coconut with the top chopped off. So that was what he had in his sack. When I thought he was leaving he'd just gone out to the veranda to get the coconut. Without a word, I gave him a mug and he tipped the coconut water in. I wanted to beg him again not to say anything to Gran, but my pride wouldn't let me. If he could ignore what I had said before, then there was no point in pleading with him now.

'You want one?'

I realized that I was staring at the coconut. To tell

you the truth, the glug-glug-glugging of the juice into the mug was making my mouth water. I adore jelly coconut, but I didn't want Maas Josh to think I was coveting Gran's.

'I don't . . .'

'Is a'right. I have plenty in the bag. You not going to rob you granny.' He put the empty coconut on the kitchen table and turned to the door. 'I will take this in to Sister Patterson and then chop one for you.'

And that's what he did. When he came back he handed me a coconut with the top chopped off, and put the sack with the rest on the kitchen floor next to the pumpkin basket.

'I shave off the top of them a'ready so when you granny want another one you just have to open it with a knife. You think you can do that?'

'Yes, Maas Josh.' I didn't bother to tell him I'd been chopping coconuts since I was nine.

'A'right, I going now. Look after you granny, you hear.'

'Yes, sir.'

Not a word about the incident at the post office. I waited for Gran to call and ask me about it. Nothing. I took her the pumpkin soup when it was ready and waited for some hint that she knew.

'That Maas Joshie is such a nice man,' was all she said.

I had to agree with her. And that was before we found out just how nice he was.

I'd just finished washing the dishes from dinner

21

when I heard another, 'Mind you dog!' It was Miss Hannah from the corner shop.

'Maas Joshie tell me you granny sick,' she said. I bring her some milk stout to build up her strength.'

By the end of the evening, seven people had come bringing fruit, vegetables and various bottled concoctions to build up granny's strength. She was exhausted by the time the last one left, and so was I. I fell asleep almost as soon as I lay down, but not before I'd made a promise to myself to buy at least three ice creams a week from Maas Josh.

In all the excitement, I completely forgot about Cousin Sophie's letter.

Chapter Four

Pastor Duncan was running a campaign to finish the church, but it wasn't going too well. People didn't like to sit still and meditate, which was all we seemed to do in our church. Today there were more people than usual because there was supposed to be a preacher from Headquarters in Kingston, come to help with the campaign. But it seemed like he'd lost his way because, although it was almost time to go home, nobody had seen him yet.

Poor Pastor Duncan was in a bit of a state as I don't think he'd prepared a sermon. He talked a little about loving one another, begged everybody to give generously to the building fund and then announced an extra long period of meditation when we were supposed to pray for the building work.

I think more people would have come if it weren't for the fact that the Pentecostal Church of God next door was having their campaign at the same time. I'd heard Aunt Phyllis telling Granny that it was bad planning by Pastor Duncan, because he well knew that the Pentecostal Church had their campaign at this same time every year. But Granny said she thought it was because Pastor Duncan wanted to catch people before they spent all their Christmas money. That's why he couldn't wait until the New Year, which would have made more sense.

Be that as it may, the Pentecostal Church was full to the brim and everybody over there looked like they were having a great time. I didn't want to be disloyal to Gran and Pastor Duncan, but I really wished I was over there too. The singing sounded so sweet and lively, unlike the kind of hymns we sang in our church. It was hard to get excited about 'Rock of Ages' when you could hear 'Don't board the wrong train' drumming in your ears.

I looked at Gran. Her head beneath the broad-rimmed black hat was bowed over her Bible. Her lips moved silently and her eyes, peering over the top of her glasses, followed her finger as it traced the lines of Psalm 97. Although she was so much better I thought she should have stayed home to rest today, but she didn't like to miss church unless she really couldn't help it.

I couldn't understand that myself. It's not as if the brethren were such exciting company. But the only time I mentioned this, Granny told me off. Said I should learn to look for the good in people and not be so negative about the brethren. Anyway she went to church to talk with her God, and not to socialize. I didn't say anything after that.

I was sitting there trying hard to pay attention to the words in my Bible, which I was supposed to be reading silently, and before I knew it my feet started twitching. The music from next door was like a sneaky snake creeping into my body and I started to stamp the red clay. I didn't even notice the dust rising or my Bible falling to the ground. My body was swaying in time to the music and, without my permission, my hands started clapping. I completely forgot that I wasn't sitting in the church next door and I shut my eyes and joined in with the singing.

'Don't board the wrong train, hallelujah, board the wrong train.'

'Behave yourself, child.'

I jumped when I heard this voice so close to my ear at the same time that I heard a loud 'Shhh!' from the rest of the congregation. Granny's man-sized hand covered up both of mine in mid-clap. It was then that I realized what I was doing. I peeked up at Gran from under the brim of my hat.

Gran's mouth was pinched tight like a drawstring purse. I looked round the wooden shack and met the disapproving stare of the entire congregation of the Church of the Holy Silence. Eleven pairs of eyes asking how I could disrupt this time of quiet meditation with such vulgar behaviour.

I glanced to the right and met Sister Walters's stare. Oh boy, I was in big trouble now. Sister Walters wouldn't miss this heaven-sent opportunity to let Gran know she wasn't 'bringing up the child properly'. And Gran didn't like anybody questioning her child-raising ability. She said after she'd brought up three of her own and all of them alive, nobody had any right to tell her how to bring up children. And especially not Sister Walters.

Actually, only two of Gran's children were still alive. My father died when I was nearly four, but I think what Granny meant was that she raised three children without losing any in childhood. That seemed to be something to be proud of round these parts.

Anyway, I would have to be on my best behaviour for the rest of the service. I bent down to take up my Bible and tried to let the silence fill my soul. I tried to feel the Spirit like Pastor Duncan had told us to do. I sat quietly, hands clasped in my lap, hoping that I was looking sufficiently penitent and that Gran would notice how hard I was trying.

But the Devil wouldn't leave me alone. He turned my eyes to the church next door. They hadn't put in the windows yet, and through the large holes in the concrete wall I could see pretty much everything that was going on.

To begin with, I satisfied myself with just a sideways glance from the corner of my eye now and then. But when I saw Miss Liz from the corner shop rolling around on the ground, I turned my head and stared. The Church of the Holy Silence didn't believe in getting in the spirit, so I had to depend on the church next door for that kind of excitement.

Suddenly my head was twisted round to face the front. Gran held on to my skull like she thought it was going to run away if she let go. Then when she was sure I was going to behave, she let her hand drop on to the Bible in her lap. I watched her hand tapping the Bible and I knew for sure I was in trouble.

As soon as Pastor Duncan dismissed the congregation, Sister Walters waddled over, her little peeny eyes staring out of the folds of fat in her face. 'Sister Patterson, I want to talk to you for a minute.'

Sister Walters used to live in England and she didn't let anyone forget it. Aunt Phyllis said her accent was more English than the English. Nadine sometimes teased me that when I went to England I would sound like Sister Walters but I told her I would cut out my tongue first.

I felt alarm flutter in my stomach now. I didn't have to ask why Sister Walters wanted a chat and I heard Gran whisper to herself, 'Lord, give me strength.' From the way her fingers were digging into my shoulder, I knew she was trying hard to control herself. But her face was perfectly pleasant when she turned to Sister Walters. She removed her hand and told me to wait for her by the side of the road.

'Just a minute, Joyanna. You might as well hear this because it concerns you.'

Sister Walters used to teach me in Sunday school and she always used my full name though I'd told her over and over that everybody called me Joy. I stopped. Although I didn't want her chastising me in front of Gran, I didn't want her slandering me behind my back either. If they were going to be talking about me I wanted to hear what they were saying. But Granny stared straight into Sister Walters's eyes and said, 'Joy, go and wait for me by the side of the road.'

I looked from Gran to Sister Walters and back at Gran. 'Yes, ma'am,' I said, and hurried down the little dirt track from the church.

All the time they were talking I was straining to hear what they were saying. There's nothing worse than knowing people are talking about you and not being able to hear what they're saying. Sister Walters started off loudly enough, telling the whole world how she was 'absolutely astonished at Joyanna's behaviour in the house of the Lord'. But although I was only about twenty yards from them, Granny kept her voice low and I couldn't hear a word she was saying. Sister Walters must've felt foolish talking so loudly when Granny was nearly whispering, so she lowered her voice too, and no matter how much I tried I couldn't hear anything else.

I let my eyes wander up to the Church of God again. It was packed as usual and I wished, not for the first time, that I belonged to that church instead of the Church of the Holy Silence. Everybody up there looked so happy, like they were on first name terms with God. They were always the last to dismiss church too, as if they didn't want to leave their friend's house. And now with this campaign going on, you could bet none of them would be going home before two o'clock.

'I am surprised to see you take that attitude, Sister

Patterson. I would have thought that you would welcome a bit of friendly advice from someone of my experience.'

I forgot about the singing and shouting next door when I heard Sister Walters's raised voice. I saw Gran look to the church doorway to see if anybody was listening, but nobody was paying any attention. After the forced silence inside, they were making up for lost time, chatting in little groups. Anyway, Sister Walters had the kind of voice that people tried to shut out rather than strained to listen to. Midway between an angry squawk and a shriek, she sounded like a screech owl trying to lay an ostrich egg.

Granny was still keeping her voice low and I tried to read her lips. I couldn't make out much but it seemed like she'd asked Sister Walters about her experience because the woman pulled herself up to her full five feet and said in a voice like she'd just finished drinking iced water, 'Let me remind you that I have been a Sunday school teacher for five years, Mrs Patterson. And even though I have no children of my own, I know only too well that children need a firm hand if they are to turn out to be any good.'

Granny said something else and then turned and started walking towards me. Sister Walters puffed out her substantial chest like a mad bullfrog. She was looking at Gran as if she wanted to do something un-Christian to her. Then she dropped the bombshell. 'If that's the way you bring her up it is no wonder the child nearly got herself killed in the street on Friday.'

Gran stopped. So did my heart. Gran turned to Sister Walters, but the woman was walking back to the church without even waiting to see what effect her words had. Gran opened her mouth, then snapped it shut without saying anything. She came slowly towards me, stopped and gazed at me as if she was seeing me for the first time. Then she carried on up the road to our house.

'Come on, child. Full time we go home.'

Oh boy. I was in b-a-a-a-d trouble.

Chapter Five

I didn't know my cousin Sophie very well. She went to England with Mama when I was four. Both of them went to train as nurses, but Cousin Sophie apparently couldn't stand the sight of all that suffering, so did a quick career U-turn and now she was working as an accountant. Apparently this job paid a lot more than nursing, so I guessed Cousin Sophie was no fool. There was a picture of her beside the one of Mama on Gran's bedside table but I'd never paid much attention to it. I'd always been more interested in the photograph of Mama, but after today I thought I would kiss Cousin Sophie's small round face in the picture in gratitude every chance I got.

I expected Granny to say something about what Sister Walters had said, but all the way home she didn't say a word. I thought that perhaps she didn't want to make a fuss in public, and guessed there would be a reckoning when we got home. As soon as we got home, though, Granny went straight into her bedroom without saying a word.

I felt a sense of doom drop like a concrete blanket over me. If Granny was not even talking, it was worse

31

than I expected. I went into my room and changed out of my church clothes. All the time while I was putting on my yard clothes, I expected to hear the summons, but there was not a sound. I went into the kitchen and started to get the dinner ready. While I was cutting up onion, scallion, thyme, tomatoes and garlic to make the sauce for the chicken, I had my ears cocked for the call. Nothing.

I put the sauce on to simmer and headed outside to pick a hot pepper from the bush under the kitchen window. I thought Granny must be having a nap. Considering how bad she had been feeling on Friday, it was a miracle she was well enough to go to church, and she was bound to be feeling tired, especially after her confrontation with Sister Walters. I knew how much Granny would have hated that little scene and I was riddled with guilt at being the cause of it.

The chicken and rice an' peas, which we'd cooked before leaving for church, were heating up in the oven, with the yam and fried plantains. The sauce was simmering on top of the stove and the salad was in the fridge. There wasn't anything else to do in the kitchen and while Granny was having her nap it didn't make any sense to keep on worrying, so I went into my bedroom to do my homework. I took my schoolbooks out of my bag and something fell at my feet. I was just bending down to pick up Cousin Sophie's letter when Gran called me.

'Joy, come in here a minute, please.'

32

I straightened, my heart pounding and the letter once again forgotten. 'Coming, Granny,' I said, but it was another full minute before I moved.

She was sitting up against the pillows with her Bible open in her hand and her glasses on the very end of her nose.

'Yes, ma'am?'

I meant to sound as if I didn't have a clue why she wanted to see me, but my voice let me down. It came out squeaky and timid like it didn't want to have anything to do with me.

'Sit down, child.'

I pulled out the stool from under the dressing table and perched on the edge.

She peered over the top of her glasses into the Bible and closed the book. Then she put her glasses on the bedside table and looked at me.

'What you doing?'

'I was just going to start me homework, Granny,' I said hopefully. Usually my homework took priority over everything else. But not this time.

'So tell me 'bout this near-death experience, no,' she invited.

Her air of casual interest didn't fool me. I recognized the calm before the storm.

'It wasn't that bad, Granny,' I protested. 'I only bump into Maas Josh handcart by accident. Sister Walters love to exaggerate too much.'

'Child, watch you mouth,' she said sharply.

I could never understand Granny's reasoning that if

33

you can't find anything good to say about someone you should keep quiet. To my mind, if you're thinking it, you might as well say it. That way you might at least warn some trusting soul to stay away from that person.

'So that's why you so jumpy when Maas Josh come round.' You couldn't hide anything from Gran. 'How it happen?'

'Well, I was coming from the post office,' I began. And then I had a stroke of genius. 'After I collect the letter from Cousin Sophie . . .'

It worked. 'Which letter?'

'I did get a letter from Cousin Sophie for you, Ma'am, but when I come home you sick and I just forget about it.'

'Well?' Gran waved her hand impatiently. 'Where the letter now?'

'In me room, ma'am. I will go and get it.'

When I returned, her glasses were once again perched on her nose in readiness. She peered over the top of them at the postmark and without looking at me she dismissed me with a little impatient wave of her hand. 'A'right. Go and do you homework now. I will finish talk to you later.'

Part of me was glad for the little delay, but another part argued that it would have been better to get it over and done with. I dreaded to think what Miss Jones was going to say about my maths homework. My brain was in no condition to fight itself through the jungle of numbers.

The smell of burning called me to the kitchen. The sauce was ruined. I'd have to start all over again and I'd have to scour the pan as well. Sunday was fast turning into my least favourite day.

This time when Granny called me I was resigned to my fate. I couldn't think of any more delaying tactics. But Gran seemed to have forgotten about my behaviour. She had something more important to think about now.

'Sit down, child.' Her voice was sad and I felt alarm flutter to life inside me.

'I sat on the stool, my hands clasped tightly between my knees. Granny continued to look at me for a long time and then she sighed. 'This letter from Sophie concern you.'

I frowned. I couldn't think what Cousin Sophie had to say that concerned me. Unless . . . And suddenly I knew. My heart felt like a giant hand was squeezing it. I could hardly get the words out. I wanted to know and yet I didn't. But why else would Cousin Sophie be writing something concerning me?

'Mama all right, ma'am?' I whispered hoarsely. 'Anything happen to her?'

'Child, just tie up you imagination for a while. Why you must always be jumping to conclusion like you is some kind of racehorse? You mother . . . everybody fine. Sophie only writing to say that they sending for you to go and join them in England.'

The relief left me feeling weak. 'But, Granny' I know that already.' I laughed. 'Mama write long time

35

to say that she sending for me as soon as I finish primary school, remember?'

Granny hissed her teeth. 'Cho, girl, close you mouth and open you ears. Who mention anything about finishing school? I mean that you mother sending for you as soon as you finish this term. That is two months' time so you better start pack.'

Chapter Six

I couldn't wait to tell Nadine. I met her at the bottom of her lane as usual on my way to school but, before I could open my mouth, she grabbed my arm.

'I bet you can't guess what happen!' Her eyes were shining and she was breathless with anticipation.

I wasn't sure I liked the way Nadine was upstaging me. I looked at her now and because I was feeling a bit disgruntled I said, 'What, somebody dead?'

She giggled. 'No, you idiot. Nobody not dead, but somebody born.'

I forgot everything else straight away.

'You mother have her baby?'

Nadine didn't know what to do with herself. She was so happy to have something important to tell me. Usually I was the one telling her news, mostly about my mother in England. Now it was her turn. She was nodding and grinning like one of those animated clowns they sold with all the other dolls at Christmas.

'Yes, she have a little girl.'

'A girl!' This was the best news. Nadine and I had been praying for a girl because Nadine already had two little brothers and we were fed up with boys. 'When she have her?'

'Yesterday, 'bout twelve o'clock.'

'When I can see her? What you all going to call her?

'Mam was so sure she was going have another boy that we only have boy names so now we have to think of something else.'

We spent the rest of the walk to school choosing and discarding names and planning how we would take the baby for walks and show her off in the district. Just as we went through the gates, the bell went and as we were trooping in, Nadine whispered, 'Guess what else?'

It was then I remembered I hadn't told her my own news yet. 'You guess what,' I said.

'What?'

'I going to England.' I was fighting hard to keep from crowing. Nadine looked at me pityingly and I could see she thought I was just trying to compete with her news.

'But I know that a'ready,' she said scornfully. 'You been telling me the same thing ever since I know you.'

Before I could explain, Miss Jones shouted out, 'Nadine Singh and Joy Patterson, please leave the talking outside.'

It was a long morning for me, I can tell you. At recess I decided not to beat about the bush. As soon as the bell went I grabbed Nadine's elbow and we headed for the door. 'Nadine,' I said. 'You know that letter I get from Cousin Sophie on Friday?'

'Mm-mm. What 'bout it?'

'Well, she write Granny to say they sending for me in December.'

Nadine stopped suddenly, blocking the doorway, and Joseph Campbell, who was behind us, bumped into the back of her.

'Gal, get out o' the way, no,' he said irritably.

'Clear off, bwoy. Why you don't look where you going? Which December?' All in the same breath with her eyes fastened to my face. I laughed and pulled her through the door. Joseph hissed his teeth and passed round us, but he didn't say anything else. He knew better than to get into a cussing match with Nadine.

'Last year December,' I said. 'Which one you think?'

'You liar! For true?'

I nodded. 'True thing. This time next year me in England nearly one whole year.'

'So which day you going?'

'The fifteenth o' December. Cousin Sophie send the ticket a'ready.'

'But, that mean you going in . . .' she took a minute to work it out. 'Only seven weeks.' Her eyes widened. 'Joy, you almost gone a'ready. You pack yet?'

We spent the rest of recess planning my wardrobe for England, although Nadine reckoned English clothes were more stylish than the ones we could get in Jamaica, so I should just buy the clothes when I got there.

Just before we went back to class, I remembered that she still had something else to tell me.

'You know you say you have something else to tell me,' I reminded her.

'Come up to the house this evening and me will show you.'

Chapter Seven

She was gorgeous. Her little eyes were dark like a blackbird's feather and when I put my finger in her tiny hand she held it so tightly I could hardly believe someone as small as that could have so much strength. She had soft black hair all over her head and her skin was pink like a baby mouse. I loved her. I wished I could take her home.

I didn't think Mrs Singh would let me hold her when she was so young, but she must have seen the longing in my eyes when I looked in the cot, because she smiled and asked if I wanted to hold her for a while.

I had never seen any baby as small as Nadine's sister. Nadine said she only weighed four and a half pounds! She was the lightest baby I had ever held, that was for sure.

'Nadine, you so lucky!' I said enviously.

'You can talk,' Nadine retorted. 'I not the one going to England.'

Mrs Singh lifted her doting gaze from the baby's face.

'Somebody going to England?'

41

Before I could open my mouth, Nadine was quick to tell her the whole story, but I didn't mind because I only had time for the baby right then. Suddenly even England didn't seem so exciting.

Once I'd seen Nadine's sister, I'd completely forgotten that Nadine had something else to show me until she said, 'I want to show you something, but come with me to the kitchen first. I have to put on the dinner.'

I didn't want to give up the baby, but I was curious, so I handed her back to Mrs Singh and followed Nadine into the kitchen. While she put the pot of water on the fire and took the yam out of the food basket to peel it, I tried to find out what she had to show me, but she just kept saying, 'Wait and see.' I've never known anybody to love a secret like Nadine. It can be so irritating sometimes.

When the food was in the pot she turned down the heat.

'All right. Come let me show you.'

I followed her to the grapefruit tree where we usually played together. We had a little playhouse that Mr Singh had built for Nadine when she was about six. It was a bit too small for her now, but we liked to squeeze ourselves in there when we wanted to be together without Nadine's two little brothers bothering us. They were at the barbershop with Nadine's father now, so I didn't think we needed to use the playhouse. But Nadine wasn't going there.

We came to a clump of sugar canes. Behind this

was an old water tank with one side missing. Sometimes we would go inside and holler. The echo would bounce off the metal wall and sound really scary, but in the hot sun it was boiling, so we didn't go in there often. I noticed that somebody had spread a piece of tarpaulin over the top. What a good idea. Now it wouldn't get so hot and we could play in there longer.

But Nadine hadn't come to play. She stood by the opening and whispered, 'Look inside.'

I bent down and looked.

'Nadine, why you didn't tell me?'

'I did want to surprise you. Don't you think them pretty?'

'Them glorious.'

Nadine's dog Bessie was lying on a sack with five fat, fluffy little puppies beside her.

'When she have them?'

'This morning.'

'You think Bessie will mind if I hold one?'

'I don't think so. She didn't say anything when I hold them.' She reached in and stroked Bessie. Then she picked up a little wriggling ball of dark brown fur and held it out to me. 'Don't you think that one look like Bessie?'

'Spitting image,' I agreed.

Bessie started to look a bit anxious and whimper so I gave the puppy back to Nadine who put it back beside its mother. Bessie licked it and nuzzled it close up to her.

''Member that you promise I could have one.' I knew exactly which one I wanted; the one that looked so much like Bessie. I'd felt my heart turn over when I'd held her. I was going to train her to sit and get things and do all kinds of tricks.

Nadine looked at me, puzzled.

'But, Joy, you going to England in December. You can't take the puppy with you.'

The sky was a sparkling hurt-your-eye blue. The sun was blazing down like it was in a competition. The red earth at my feet was baked hard till it cracked and the grass was brown as parched corn. Even the sugar cane leaves were curling brown in the heat. But I felt cold.

She was right. I wouldn't have enough time to train the puppy. It would probably just be ready to leave Bessie by the time I left. I would never see Nadine's baby sister growing up. I wouldn't go with Nadine to the comprehensive school. I probably wouldn't see Gran again after I left. All the time I had been thinking about going to England, I'd never thought about leaving Jamaica.

'I think I better go home now,' I said quietly. 'Granny must be wondering what happen to me.'

Chapter Eight

Only the first day of the half-term holiday and already I was bored to distraction. Trouble was, it was so hot that even the bees were too sleepy to buzz. I was sitting on the veranda hoping to catch any stray breeze that was passing, but it seemed every one was on vacation. I was idly watching the insects fly drowsily between the hibiscus and the ixora flowers. Their droning was half-hearted, like a broken-down aeroplane, coming in fits and starts.

I slouched in Granny's rocking chair, contemplating the idea of going to have another cold shower. It was only eleven and I'd already had two, but my clothes were sticking to my skin again. It was hard to believe it was nearly the end of October. This was more like the middle of August. I couldn't remember it ever being so hot this time of year.

When Nadine came up the path to the house with a plastic bag under her arm, I couldn't have been happier to see her.

'You want go swim?' she asked. 'You might not get another chance before you fly.'

It was the best suggestion I had heard for a while.

'Sure,' I said. I gestured to the plastic bag she was carrying. 'What you got?'

Nadine opened it, her eyes darting around to make sure we were alone. Inside was a cooking pan, a bottle of coconut oil and a salted mackerel. A secret cookout. Nadine had some great ideas sometimes.

'I will get the matches and the kerosene oil to light the fire.' I headed into the house.

'And bring a knife for the breadfruit,' Nadine said. 'I forget mine.'

Granny was washing clothes in the wash-pan under the grapefruit tree. 'I going down the gully with Nadine, Granny,' I called out to her and we scooted before she could think about it and object. Granny didn't like us wandering the bushes on our own. She thought we should always be doing something useful because 'the Devil find work for idle hands'.

The gully was a stream, which flowed round the boundary of Granny's land. It was about a quarter of a mile downhill from the house. Halfway there we stopped to get some tomatoes, garlic, thyme and an onion from Granny's vegetable plot.

'I wish I did bring the machete,' I said. 'I could dig a yam to roast with the breadfruit.'

'And we could use it to chop wood for the fire,' Nadine agreed.

'You want to go back for it?'

We both looked back the way we'd come. Perspiration was pouring down our faces and turning our clothes into second skins. Neither of us fancied climbing the hill again just yet. Besides, Granny might find me something to do if I went back. 'We will manage,' I said.

When we got to the gully, I was all for dashing into the water straight away, but Nadine said we should put the breadfruit on to roast first, then we could swim while it was cooking. She went to get the firewood while I climbed the breadfruit tree and picked two of the best breadfruits I could find. The breadfruit tree marked the spot where Granny's land ended and Miss Daphne's began. As if to emphasize this, Miss Daphne had built a hut almost leaning against it.

We lit the fire at the foot of the tree, nearest the hut. That way it would be sheltered from any wind that might decide to puff past. Once the fire was blazing away, we put the breadfruits on to roast and I strolled the few yards to the gully to fill the cooking pan with water. We dropped in the mackerel, put it on the fire and I started to cut up the seasoning for the fish. As we hadn't brought any plates with us, I cut two leaves from one of the banana trees nearby. These would do for both plate and table.

'Know what would be nice?' Nadine asked.

I looked up, my eyes streaming from cutting up the onion.

'A ripe pear,' she said. 'That's what this cookout need. A nice ripe avocado pear.'

I pointed towards a clump of cocoa trees. 'If you go through there you will see a black skin pear tree. See if any drop.'

'A'right. I will get some more wood too. You watch the breadfruit.'

I had the bright idea while she was gone, to try and catch some janga, shrimps, or a crayfish to surprise Nadine. She loves shellfish, though I'm not too particular to them myself.

The janga weren't very cooperative. I saw a couple of shrimps flit through the water, their translucent shells hardly visible – just a flash like a shadow and then they were gone. I was balancing on top of a large rock, my hand up to my elbow, feeling underneath the rock for crayfish, when Nadine gave a loud yell. I jumped, lost my balance and toppled over into the gully. I got up spluttering and ready to give Nadine a piece of my mind, when I saw that the thatch from Miss Daphne's hut was blazing merrily away.

I raced up to the hut as fast as I could with my wet skirt clinging to my legs and the water dripping out of my hair trying to blind me. By the time I got there Nadine had taken off her shorts and was beating at the roof with them. All it did was fan the fire.

'Nadine, stop!' I shouted. 'You making it worse.' I grabbed the shorts from her and spun them round my hand. Then I lifted the pan with the mackerel off the fire and flung the water at the roof. Most of it, including the mackerel, fell on the ground by the side of the hut, but a little reached the roof. The fire spluttered, protesting, before recovering. It had eaten nearly half the roof by now.

48

I thrust the pan at Nadine. 'Here, you go fill this in the gully, I going to beat it with me skirt.'

'But you just say . . .'

'My skirt wet, Nadine. Make haste, no.'

She grabbed the pan, and then dropped it, yelping with pain.

'Oh, sorry. I forget it hot. Here, use this. I unwrapped her shorts from my hand and thrust them at her. Ignoring her killer look, I took off my skirt and started beating at the flames with it. With that and the pans of water Nadine brought from the gully, we managed to save a tiny bit of Miss Daphne's roof. It was lucky that the rest of the hut was made from zinc, or we'd have probably lost the whole thing.

I gazed dolefully round our campsite. The two half-roasted breadfruits looked quite forlorn in the smouldering ashes. They were still glistening from the water Nadine had doused them with when she slipped on the ripe avocado pear she'd found, as she was returning from one of her trips to the gully. The breadfruit tree itself was charred on the side nearest to the hut, the lower leaves curling and black.

'I think you was going to watch the fire?' Nadine said.

'I did just go to catch some shrimps for you. I was only gone two minutes. The breeze must o' change direction.' Then I noticed the empty kerosene oil bottle on the ground.

'Nadine,' I screeched. 'You idiot! You throw the

49

whole o' the oil on the fire? No wonder you burn down Miss Daphne hut.'

'I never. You think me a fool?'

I took up the empty bottle and thrust it under her nose. 'So what happen to the oil?'

'Well when me come back the fire did look like it out. Me just put some more wood on it and me was going put a little oil on it to light it again when a mosquito bite me and make me drop the bottle.'

'I put my arm round her and together we sat down on the grass, ignoring the scratchiness of the mimosa weeds against our bare thighs.

'And that mackerel cost so much.' I felt guilty at the deep regret in her voice.

'We could wash it in the gully and eat it,' I offered. 'It still good.'

Nadine gave me a scornful look. 'Yeah right. You can eat it.'

I looked towards the mackerel where it lay in pieces on a bed of old goat's droppings. I suddenly lost my appetite.

'What we going to do?'

Nadine considered for a minute. 'If we leave now, nobody will know is we,' she suggested.

Immediately Granny's voice came into my head. 'Speak the truth and speak it ever, cost it what it will, he who hides the wrong he did, does the wrong thing still.' It was all right for Nadine. She didn't live with a sixty-seven-year-old conscience.

'No we can't do that,' I said. 'But maybe we could

cut some coconut bough and put it back on. Then they might not notice.'

'Oh, yeah.' Nadine pointed to the basket I'd brought the things in. 'That little knife you have will cut coconut bough really good.'

She was right; it was a stupid idea. If only we'd gone back for the machete. We sat like that, our heads in our hands, miserably considering what our families were going to say and do when they found out, and racking our brains to try and find a way out.

'Mam going kill me,' Nadine mourned.

'Dog nyam me supper too,' I said. We were silent then, Nadine probably trying to concoct a story to get us out of trouble, me wondering how many of our classmates would come to our funerals.

'I suppose we better clear up,' Nadine said at last.

'And we better go wash out we clothes them.'

We got up and went to the gully. Without soap, we just seemed to make them worse. Nadine's pale pink shorts were now a dirty grey with a big hole burned in the back where the fire had eaten the cloth when I'd used them as an oven glove. My blue-and-white floral wrap-around skirt was a sick-looking greyish black. We'd have a hard time going undetected in these. Since our tops were in little better state, we washed those as well. We spread them on two large boulders to dry in the hot sun and went to clear up the mess.

Nadine was collecting the pan and I was using a broom of twigs to sweep dirt on to the fire. Although

51

it looked well and truly dead, I wasn't taking the chance. We both had our bottoms stuck into the air with nothing on but our underwear.

'What going on here?'

Just like in those films, Nadine and I froze, then looked round in slow motion. We were presenting a perfect view of our skimpily clad rear ends to Miss Daphne. She didn't look very impressed with the spectacle.

I glanced helplessly at Nadine. Her face and hair were streaked with ashes and soot, her hair singed, her short fringe clinging in damp rats' tails to her forehead, her elbows and knees still muddy from her fall. I suspected that I did not look much better. Slowly we stood up and turned to face Miss Daphne.

'Oh, Lord, we dead now,' Nadine whispered.

And we hadn't even had a swim.

Chapter Nine

'Hold still, chile, you nearly make me stick the pin into you.'

Nearly! My back already felt like a pincushion. Why Granny had to make me a new dress now, I didn't know. It wasn't like Mama hadn't sent me enough clothes from England. But I think Gran didn't want Mama to think I wasn't being looked after properly. So the first thing she did after reading Cousin Sophie's letter was to go to the market and make the cloth-seller rich. She'd been sewing since and now, with only one day before I was to leave, you'd think she would give it a rest. It wasn't as if I didn't have more important things to do. I really didn't want to spend my last full day in Jamaica inside, being stuck full of pins.

'Joyanna,' Granny said with a sigh. She looked at me like someone about to deliver bad news.

Oh-oh, I thought. Whenever Granny used my full name like that, it was because she had something important to say. Important to her, that is. More than likely embarrassing, or worse, painful, for me.

She'd used that same tone after Miss Daphne had

marched Nadine and I into the yard and called Gran to come and witness our total humiliation. You'd think the woman could have at least waited until our clothes had dried. But no, we had to walk all the way home, dripping, with our faces still looking like something out of a horror movie. Poor Nadine had to walk through the bush with a big hole in the seat of her shorts where the fire had eaten the cloth. In our haste to get to the gully, we'd forgotten to take any towels, so she didn't even have one to cover her shame.

'Joyanna,' Granny had said when she'd finished apologizing and Miss Daphne had taken Nadine home (though not before Granny had promised to send somebody to fix the hut roof). 'Come inside.'

Nadine and I were not allowed to see each other for the rest of the half-term, which I thought was really mean considering that I got the worst telling-off in my life, had to take a basket of yams and breadfruits to Miss Daphne as a peace offering and apologize all over again even though I'd already said sorry a million times by the river and another million times in the yard.

Nadine wouldn't discuss her punishment with me, but from the way her face snapped shut when I asked her, I got the impression it wasn't too pleasant.

It was also the tone Granny used when I was in trouble. Now I tried to think what I'd done, but for once my conscience was clear.

'You mother ask me to let you know, although I think is her place to tell you.'

Oh boy, now I knew what she was going to say. She had used the same words the time she decided I should know about growing up and bodily changes. 'Is really you mother place to tell you these things, but you getting to be a young lady now.' And then had followed the most embarrassing and confusing ten minutes of my life. Luckily we'd learned all about that from the school nurse or there'd be one confused child going to England, I can tell you. She had obviously forgotten she had done it before and was going to do it all again! I groaned.

'Is like this . . .'

'Hold you dog.'

Through the open bedroom window we saw Cousin Elaine climbing up the steps on to the veranda. She was Aunt Phyllis's and Uncle Ben's only daughter. I breathed a sigh of relief when I saw her. She couldn't have timed it better. With any luck Granny would have forgotten again by the time she left.

I noticed Cousin Elaine's cornrows straight away. They spiralled to the top of her head where they ended in a kind of topknot, so she looked like she was wearing a crown. I thought it suited her perfectly. She was sixteen, tall and slim with large coal-black eyes and a mouth that looked like it was always about to break into a smile. Uncle Ben said she reminded him of Cleopatra. I guess that's why he called her Princess.

'Eh-Eh,' Granny said. 'Elaine, you early. Come inside.'

'Morning, Granny, hi, Joy. You ready for me to do your hair?'

'You come too soon, Elaine,' I told her. 'I didn't even have a chance to take out me plaits yet.'

'Don't worry 'bout that. I will take them out.'

'You going to do mine like yours?' I asked hopefully.

She laughed and patted her head dismissively. 'This old style? No, you need something special to go to England with. I have just the style for you.' She put the carrier bag she was carrying on the table and slid on to the dressing-table stool. 'Mam send something for you to take to Aunt Aimee. She would o' bring them over this evening, but she say you probably want to pack them.'

I eyed the bag trying to guess what was in it, but I couldn't get a clue.

'What in it?' I asked.

'Just some sorrel and a Christmas cake Mam bake.'

'Mmm.' I grinned at my cousin, drooling at the thought of Aunt Phyllis's Christmas cake. Granny always said Auntie made the best Christmas cake in the district. In the whole island, I thought. I turned to Gran. 'Mama will love that, eh, Granny?'

Granny must be losing her hearing as well as her memory because she acted like she hadn't heard. 'A'right, you can take it off now,' she said. She folded the half-made dress on top of the sewing machine and turned to Elaine. 'Tell you mother thanks for me, and tell her to come early tonight to help me with the punch.' And then she went into the kitchen.

56

'So,' Elaine said when we were in my bedroom and she was brushing my hair. 'You ready for your send-off?'

'Ehn-ehn. But me can't believe a time for me to go a'ready. Look like just yesterday Cousin Sophie send the ticket and now tomorrow this time me going be on me way to England.'

'How come Sophie send the ticket instead o' Aunt Aimee?'

'I ask Granny the same question, but until now I don't know what she say. You know how Granny can change the subject when she don't want to answer you. But who cares? Me going to England and that's all me care 'bout.'

'Me no blame you. But I going to miss you, chile.'

'Not as much as I going to miss you,' I told her. 'Who going to cornrow me hair? I only hope Mama know how to do it. If she plait hair like Granny, me dead.'

She laughed. 'Don' worry. Cousin Sophie will do it for you. She used to plait mine before she left.'

I clasped my hands over my heart, raised my eyes heavenward and sighed with relief. 'Thank you, Lord.'

Still laughing, Cousin Elaine asked, 'So you know who and who coming tonight?'

'No. I was hoping Uncle Bob would o' come back from Miami in time, but it look like I not going to see him before I leave. Most o' them who coming is

57

Granny friend, I bet. They not really coming to say goodbye to me, is just a excuse to have a party.'

'You too cynical. People in the district like you. They all going be sorry to see you go.'

'Oh sure,' I scoffed. 'Maas Josh going be crying him eyes out.'

Elaine spluttered. 'Most people get into car accidents, only you could end up in a cart accident.'

'I bet Miss Daphne going be real sorry too,' I said dryly.

This time Elaine gave a hoot of laughter. 'I wish I could o' see you and that fire.' She started flapping her arms and blowing on an imaginary fire.

'It never funny,' I said, but I couldn't help giggling. Cousin Elaine looked so silly and though it was dire at the time, I could see the funny side of it now.

'She should o' thank me and Nadine,' I said. 'The roof Uncle Ben put on her hut ten times better than the one we burn down.'

'Maybe she will remember to thank you tonight,' Elaine said. She licked her lips. 'Papa making some wicked rum punch and I can't wait to sample it.'

'Elaine! Uncle Ben don't allow you to drink rum?'

'Who say I going to tell him?'

But Cousin Elaine is all mouth sometimes. I know for certain she didn't taste a drop of rum punch that night. I don't know why anybody would want to drink that horrible smelling stuff when the pure fruit punch taste so nice anyway.

Uncle Ben fixed up some loudspeakers and the

music swelled through the yard and burst out over the whole of Prospect. It drew people the way ripe mangoes attract bees and in no time the yard was full of people, half of them I'm sure Granny hadn't even invited. Uncle fitted light bulbs on to the outside of the veranda so that the whole yard was bathed in light and it felt like carnival.

Nadine came with her dad. Mrs Singh didn't want to leave the children, especially the baby, so late at night. Nadine started eyeing the plates of curry goat in people's hands straight away. I had to laugh. Sometimes I think she's got a bottomless pit for a stomach. I could never understand how she stayed so slim when she went through food like a bulldozer through a road bank.

I grabbed her hand and headed through the crowd to the kitchen. 'Come on, I know what you want.' Aunt Phyllis and Gran were supervising the food.

'Oh, look, the girl herself.' Aunt Phyllis reached for a plate and started piling on rice and curry goat. The higher she piled it, the bigger Nadine's eyes grew. 'A'right, who first?'

'Give it to Nadine,' I said. 'I can't eat that much.'

'Eh-eh, chile, you better eat up, you hear. This might have to last you a long time till you get used to the England food.' But she passed it to Nadine who didn't complain. We sat on the grass with our backs against the tangerine tree and tucked in.

The curry goat was peppery and my tongue was tingling. I could really have done with a fruit punch to cool it down, but I didn't fancy battling my way back into the kitchen just yet. I was raising the last forkful of rice to my mouth when I looked up and the fork fell on to the plate again. I nudged Nadine who was tucking in like she hadn't seen food for days.

'Look!' I whispered. 'What him think him doing?'

Nadine followed my pointing finger and her mouth dropped open to display half-chewed rice and curry to all who cared to see. Not pretty. I turned again to where Maas Josh was wheeling his handcart into the yard. Surely he wasn't intending to sell his ice cream at Gran's party? He stopped, looked around until our eyes met. He hurried over, face creased into a beaming smile.

'Evening, Miss Joy,' he said. 'When Sister Patterson invite me to you send-off, I didn't know what to bring. But then I say to meself, "I know how Miss Joy love ice cream. And as the weather so hot," I say to meself, "I bet Miss Joy wouldn't mind some ice cream." So this,' he rubbed his hand over the ice-cream bucket, 'is for you an' you guest them tonight.'

I didn't know where to look. I couldn't remember being so touched in my whole life. And so ashamed. I should have remembered how nice Maas Josh had been when Gran was ill. Thank goodness I hadn't said anything.

'Wow! Cool!' Nadine cried through a mouthful of rice and curry.

'Thank you, Maas Josh,' I mumbled.

'That's a'right, Miss Joy. You want me to serve you guest them or you want to do that youself?'

Well, you should have seen me and Nadine serving ice cream. You should have heard us shouting, 'Come an' get you ice cre-e-e-am! Best ice cream in town!' You should have seen us tucking into the biggest ice creams we ever had. Just the thing for a tongue tingling from too much spicy curry goat.

I left Nadine in charge while I went to get some food for Maas Josh. I made sure Granny piled the plate really high and I found the biggest glass for his rum punch.

The old people – Gran, Maas Josh, Miss Daphne and the others – cleared a space and Uncle Ben put on some old-time music. Nadine and I perched in the tangerine tree to watch the quadrille and the dinky minny, dances you didn't see much any more (I *knew* this send-off was just an excuse). Then Uncle put on some more lively music. It was still old-time; folk songs and so on, because Granny, being a church woman, wouldn't allow reggae in her yard because most of the lyrics talk about all the things that Pastor warned against. But Uncle did sneak in a few old, old reggae pieces and some ska, from I don't know when. So all the young people including me and Nadine had plenty to dance to.

By the time Mr Singh came to tell Nadine it was time to go, I was nearly dropping from tiredness myself. 'See you tomorrow,' Nadine said.

'Yeah, see you tomorrow.' The thought came to me

that this was the last time I would say that to Nadine. But I pushed it to the back of my mind. I wouldn't spoil my last few hours in Jamaica by thinking about that.

Chapter Ten

I'd been to the airport before, when Mama was going to England with Cousin Sophie. I barely remembered anything because I'd been only four at the time, but I remembered the noise. I remembered the loud scream of the engines as the planes landed or took off; the shouts of the porters ordering people to clear the way for the trolleys full of luggage; the yells of joy and excitement as people caught the first glimpse of visiting relatives and friends; and the bawling as people said goodbye.

I didn't remember the heat though. Back in the country, we were just beginning to feel the cool Christmas breeze blowing across the mountains. But here in Kingston it was like the middle of the dry season. Hot and sticky. I was burning up in the long-sleeved dress and the nylon stockings that Granny had insisted I wear. She said Sophie had written that it was cold over there and she didn't want me to go to England and catch a chill. I was stifling.

The dress was from England. High-necked, dark blue and made out of wool. I just knew I was going to be well roasted before I got there. It had a blue jacket to match but Granny said I could carry it till I arrived. I knew I wouldn't need it at all, but I didn't say anything. I could see Granny was upset. She pretended she had something in her eye, but I wasn't fooled. That is the oldest trick. Besides, I was feeling just the same. That is why I wasn't saying anything much. My throat was too tight and burning to let any words through.

We'd travelled up to the airport in Uncle Ben's car with Aunt Phyllis, my cousin Elaine and Nadine. Mrs Singh hadn't been too sure about Nadine missing school, but in the end she'd decided that the extra time we'd have together was more important.

Friday had been my last day at school. The class had made a scrapbook for me with their self-portraits and a little message from everybody. Miss Jones had made a speech wishing me well and saying she hoped I wouldn't forget them and Nadine and Herma Johnson nearly washed away the classroom with eyewater. I'd expected that Nadine would end up crying, but I was surprised to see Herma so upset. It was not like we were best friends or anything.

I'd promised myself I wouldn't cry and I plastered a plastic smile on my face all the way though Miss Jones's speech. When Herma started to cry, I felt a little knot in my throat, but I was still all right until Nadine started. And then the water tank behind my eyelids burst. When Johnny Mundle shouted out, 'Say howdy-do to the Queen for me,' everybody laughed and I tried to laugh with them, but I ended up just blubbing even harder. I was really cross with myself and it didn't help that I could see that Miss Jones and most of the girls in the class were also fighting back tears. Goodbyes are terrible.

And now that we didn't have long before I boarded the plane, I was dreading the final goodbye. We were all standing together in the lounge and I had so much I wanted to say, but I didn't trust my voice.

It was time to go. I said goodbye to Aunt Phyllis and Uncle Ben first. Auntie hugged me tight, tight, kissing me over and over until Elaine pulled her away.

'Hey, save some for the rest of we, Mama.' She was laughing, but she was also blinking really fast. 'If anybody in England admire you fancy hairstyle, make sure you give them me address.' She patted the cornrows that she'd spent two hours putting in my hair.

Elaine hadn't been joking when she'd said she was going to do something special. She'd plaited a quarter of the hair really finely and brought it forward over my left eye, then flicked it back into a roll, which came down to curl against my cheek. The other three quarters she'd plaited towards the centre of my head and pleated downwards, so it ended in a single plait at the back. It was the best style Elaine had ever done for me.

She stepped back now and I turned to Nadine. 'Make sure you answer me letter them when me write, you hear. I know you and writing can't agree.'

'You just make sure you write, that's all.' We

hugged as if we'd never let each other go. Nadine whispered into my ear. 'And don't forget that we still best friend no matter where you go.'

I patted her on the shoulder. 'Last lick,' I said. It was a stupid thing to do. I suddenly thought it could really be a 'last lick' because I didn't know if I would ever see Nadine again. My whisper was low and hoarse and I was thinking she maybe hadn't heard, but when I looked into her face I could see that she had. I turned away quickly.

Granny didn't say anything. She just hugged me till my ribs started screaming for mercy. I couldn't say anything either, and it wasn't just because of my ribs. I followed Miss Helen, the stewardess who would be looking after me on the flight. I turned back once to wave. Nadine had a tissue over her mouth and tears were streaming down her face like a river. Uncle Ben, Aunt Phyllis and Elaine each had a crooked smile as they waved. Granny raised her hand, but she didn't wave. She just stood there looking at me with her hand raised in the air like she didn't know what to do with it. I couldn't look back after that.

Part Two:

ENGLAND

Chapter Eleven

It was lucky that I had the stewardess to look after me because I'm sure if I was on my own I would still be walking around Heathrow now trying to find my way out. I'd never seen anywhere as big as that. I was trying to look sophisticated and as if I was used to being in a place like this, but when I saw a woman looking at me and smiling I realized that I had my mouth wide open. I snapped it shut and kept my eyes on Miss Helen after that.

'Now let's see if we can find your mum.' Miss Helen smiled at me as we put my suitcases on the trolley with hers. I smiled back but I think she could see I was nervous because she took my hand and squeezed it. 'It's going to be all right, you'll see.'

But it wasn't all right. I couldn't see Mama anywhere. I looked all over the crowd for a plump, brown woman with a beaming smile, but she wasn't there. And then my eyes swivelled back to someone I'd just skimmed over. A tall, young woman just a bit darker than Mama, milk chocolate rather than honey. Her eyes were almost black, and they were staring at me as if they couldn't believe what they were seeing.

She started walking towards me and my heart flipped over and stopped beating for a minute. I knew for certain that something had happened to Mama. I could feel it. That's why she was not here to meet me. That's why Cousin Sophie had come instead. Now I understood what Granny had been trying to tell me yesterday. Please no. Not that!

'Cousin Sophie!'

'Joy!' She hugged me like she didn't ever want to let me go. She just kept repeating my name over and over. 'Joy, Joy, Joy.' I guessed she was glad to see me.

She held me a little way from her, her eyes sparkling like Christmas lights. 'Let me look at you. You are so BIG!'

I waited until we thanked Miss Helen and said goodbye to her before I asked the one question on my mind.

'Cousin Sophie, where Mama? Why she don't come to meet me?'

We were walking out of the airport building when I asked her, but Cousin Sophie stopped and stared. She was trying to say something, but I could tell she didn't know how to say it. One hand was twisting the strap of her handbag and the other was fidgeting on the handle of the trolley.

'Something happen to Mama? What happen to her?'

Sophie looked surprised and then she laughed a nervous little laugh. 'No, no, nothing's wrong. Aunt Aimee is fine.'

'So why she never come and meet me?'

'She's dying to see you, of course, but she couldn't get the time off work today. But don't worry, you'll see her later.'

I was nearly weak with relief, but I was curious. 'You didn't have no trouble to get time off to come and meet me?' I asked.

She smiled. 'I had some leave owing to me. I decided now was as good a time as any to take it. I can show you the sights while Aunt Aimee is at work.'

'Oh, thank you, Cousin Sophie,' I said timidly. Now that the scare was over, I suddenly felt shy to talk to her. All the time in my head I had seen how Mama and I would meet and start chatting about everything under the sun straight away. But Cousin Sophie was like a stranger to me. She looked a lot like her photograph, but she talked like Sister Walters and Miss Helen. She didn't talk like a Jamaican any more. I followed her out of the terminal, hoping and praying that Mama was not as English as Cousin Sophie; that she was still the mother I remembered from when I was four.

I'd been a bit cold in the airport, but not as cold as when I'd been in the plane. I still had on my jacket. I saw the sun shining outside and I couldn't wait to get out and warm myself in it. But when we got out into the open I felt as though somebody had just emptied a bucket of icy water over me. I sucked in my breath and stood stock still, stiff with shock. Then I turned round and bolted back inside. There was no way I was going out in that. In all my born days I never knew there was such a thing as cold sunshine.

Cousin Sophie hurried in after me and held me close to her, rubbing her hands up and down my arms to heat them up.

'I'm sorry, Joy. I was so anxious to see you I completely forgot the coat and gloves I brought for you. They're in the car. You wait here and I'll go and get them. You'll be all right on your own for a few minutes. I won't be long.'

I just nodded. When she came back she was carrying a blue coat, a scarf, woolly hat and a pair of gloves to match. She helped me to put them on. I wasn't sure I liked looking and feeling like a parcel, but I have to admit I did feel warmer as soon as I buttoned up the coat.

Before we got home, it started to rain. One minute an anaemic sun was giving us a sheepish grin, the next minute the windscreen wiper was swishing back and forth. I was listening out for the thunder but I didn't hear a sound. I waited for the rain to pick up speed and start falling properly, but it just carried on with its sulky drizzle like the sky didn't want to send any water down to earth but somebody was forcing it to. The whole place looked grey and, although the little clock on the dashboard of Cousin Sophie's red car was saying two-thirty, it looked like night was falling.

We'd left London behind and had been driving for about two hours when Cousin Sophie turned into a driveway.

'Here we are. Welcome to 21 Oakridge Avenue. We'll leave the cases in the car for the minute. Come and see your new home.'

I followed her up the flight of five steps and looked round while she scrabbled about in her handbag for her keys to open the door. So this was where my letters had been coming for the last year or so. Most of the front yard was concrete, but right next to the house somebody must have been trying to make a garden because there was a little plot of earth with things that looked like they used to be plants. Most of them looked dead though. Over to the left there was a tree, but it was dead as well. That's the thing I'd noticed all the way back from the airport. Most of the trees in England were dead. If Cousin Sophie didn't hurry up and open the door, I would be dead as well. I didn't know how anyone could survive in this weather.

At last she finished fighting with the lock and the door swung open. We stepped into a wide hallway with a flight of stairs leading up to a blue door I could just glimpse at the top. Good, I always wanted to live in a house with stairs. I started heading for the staircase, but Cousin Sophie moved over to the door in front of us.

'This is my place. Aunt Aimee has the top flat. We were very lucky to get this place.' She smiled. 'The house we shared in London was half the size of this and twice the price. That's why we had to get out of the city – too expensive, and it felt like we were living in the shed back home.' She pushed the door open and stepped back so I could walk in.

'Aunt Aimee and I both fell in love with this flat, but since . . . well, Aimee's flat is a bit small for me. Welcome home.'

The door opened into a passageway. Cousin Sophie opened another door and we stepped into a huge room. It was cold. Through the French windows I could see another dead tree and a long stretch of grass. Nothing more, except the rain.

'Come, I'll light the fire. I'm so sorry I forgot about the heating. It's set to go off when I go to work and I completely forgot to override the timer before I left. But don't worry, the flat will warm up quite soon.'

'You have a fire in you house?' I was thrilled. I forgot about the cold for a minute. I couldn't believe it. A real fire! When I used to read about log fires and chestnuts roasting at Christmas, I used to wish we had a fire in Granny's house, although I couldn't understand how it wouldn't burn the house down. And now here I was in England in Cousin Sophie's living room watching her light a real fire.

'Actually it's only imitation,' Cousin Sophie said. 'Not the real thing.'

I couldn't help feeling a little disappointed.

'Here, let me take your coat and things.'

She was taking off her coat while she was talking and then stretched out her hand for mine. I unwound the scarf and handed it to her, slowly. Then I took off my hat and handed it to her, slowly. I left the coat till last. It was thick and cumbersome, but it was warm and I didn't want to get out of it. I undid the buttons one by one, slowly. I handed it to her and she smiled and nodded towards the fire.

'Right, that should warm you up in no time. I'll go and hang these up and then we'll have a nice hot drink, OK?'

'OK.'

I watched her leave the room. Then I dived down on the carpet and stretched out my hands and feet towards the fire. All the time in Jamaica when I'd read about England in winter, I'd never dreamed it could be this cold. I was trying to stop the shivering, but it was like I'd lost control of my body. My teeth were rattling like red peas in a jam jar.

'Don't put your feet so close to the fire, Joy. You might get chilblains.'

'What's chilblains?'

'A very painful swelling on your hands and feet. You get it when you're cold and you get too close to the heat. Here, put on this jumper. It will warm you up.'

I took the jumper from Cousin Sophie and pulled it over my head. It was big and bulky and itchy.

'Now, what would you like to drink? Tea? Coffee?'

'Tea, please.'

I wondered what kind of tea she was making. I only hoped it was chocolate tea and not one of those bush teas that Granny liked to boil. I couldn't bear it if she brought me cerasee tea. It might be good for the blood but it sure was bad for my taste buds. I was thinking maybe I should have asked for coffee tea, but Granny didn't like me drinking that because all that caffeine is supposed to be bad for your heart.

When she came back, Cousin Sophie was carrying a tray with two cups, a teapot, milk jug and a plate of cookies. She offered me a cookie and then she poured out the tea. It wasn't chocolate tea. I didn't like the smell of it. It reminded me of the bush tea Granny used to give me on Sunday mornings to purge out my insides.

Cousin Sophie poured the tea and added some milk from the milk jug. I waited for her to sweeten it but she just handed it over to me. I thought she must have put the sugar in the pot before she put in the tea, so I took a big gulp. I had to hold me breath while I drank because the thing smelled too much like medicine. I got such a shock when I swallowed the tea. It was almost as bitter as cerasee, and tasted like rusty nails.

Granny always said it's bad manners to show distaste for any food somebody offer you, but the shock caught me off guard and Cousin Sophie could plainly see the way I was screwing up my face.

'Oh, did you want some sugar in that? I'm sorry; because I don't use sugar myself I sometimes forget that other people do. I'll go and get it.'

My jaw dropped. I couldn't believe anybody could drink *that* without sugar. When she came back she had a bowl of sugar and a teaspoon with her. I thought that it would need more than that little bowl of sugar to make this tea drinkable, and I was just about to put in the fifth spoonful when I looked up to see Cousin Sophie staring at me with her mouth wide open. I thought perhaps she didn't have much sugar and she didn't want me to use too much of it, so I put it back.

'Do you always use so much sugar in you tea, Joy?' she asked.

'Well,' I said, 'It depends. If it's Milo, Ovaltine or chocolate tea, I only put in one spoonful because I usually make it with condensed milk, but if it's bush tea I use two or three spoon. If it's cerasee, I need four or five spoonful to hide the taste. I never have this kind of tea before, but it taste a bit like ccrasee to me.'

Cousin Sophie looked at me for a minute like she didn't understand English and then she started to laugh. I didn't know why she was laughing, but it looked like she was laughing at me and I didn't like it. She saw my face and stopped. She shuffled up close to me on the settee, put her arm round my shoulder and kissed me on my forehead. Just like she thought I was a little baby.

'I'm sorry, Joy. I'm so stupid. I completely forgot. When we say "tea" in England, we're talking about black tea, not just any hot drink like in Jamaica. If you want chocolate tea, you ask for hot chocolate. Coffee tea is just plain coffee and tea is this stuff.'

'So what you all call bush tea?'

'Well, horrible tea, I guess. Although you don't just

go outside and pick some leaves to make a drink like you do in Jamaica. These come in packets from the supermarket. My word, I haven't heard the name cerasee since I left Jamaica.'

Horrible tea? What a strange name!

She took the cup from me. 'You don't have to drink this. Would you prefer some hot chocolate instead? I'm afraid I haven't got any Milo or Ovaltine.'

'I don't want to put you to any trouble, Cousin Sophie, I will drink the tea. It shouldn't be too bad with the sugar.'

'It's no trouble at all. So would you prefer hot chocolate or horrible tea?'

'Hot chocolate, please.' No way me coming to England to drink bush tea, especially bush tea with a name like that.

Cousin Sophie headed for the door.

'One hot chocolate coming up. And when you've had that it should be warm enough for me to show you round the flat. I won't be a minute.'

But she must have been a lot longer than a minute. The fire was warming up the room really nicely. I was watching the rain through the glass and everything outside was looking cold, grey and really dismal. But inside was warm and cosy. My eyelids started to droop and I don't know when, but sometime before cousin Sophie came back I was stretched out on the sofa fast asleep.

Chapter Twelve

I'm dreaming that Granny and I are shelling gungu peas in the kitchen. I'm looking for the 'pretty' peas, the ones that, instead of being plain green, have patterns in red, brown, black and yellow on them. It's good luck when you find them, but every time I open the shell, all I find are little, green, wriggly worms. I'm getting really upset about this and I tell Granny I'm not shelling any more. I get up from the table just as somebody shouts, 'Hold you dog!' I run out on to the veranda and I see Aunt Phyllis and Sister Walters coming up the steps.

They walk past like they haven't even seen me and then Granny comes and tells me to go to my room because the big people have important things to talk 'bout. They're talking in the front room but I can hear them from where I'm lying on my bed. They're whispering as if they don't want me to hear what they're saying, but every word is clear to me.

'She sounds so old. I haven't heard that kind of language for a long time.'

'Well what you expect? She been living with a old woman for seven years.'

'I suppose. It was still a shock though.' A pause. 'She doesn't know yet, you know'.

'What? You granny don't tell her?' That is Aunt Phyllis.

'Doesn't seem like it. Probably forgotten. You can see the state of her memory from her letters these days.'

I don't know what's happened to Sister Walters's voice. In my dream it sounds huskier and nicer to listen to. Aunt Phyllis starts talking again.

'You know, I think we should wait until she settle down a bit before we tell her. Could be a bit much for her to take in. I just think she need a little time to adjust.' There is a long pause and then Sister Walters sighs.

'I suppose you're right. We'll leave things as they are for the time being, but not too long, OK?'

'No, not too long. I can't believe the little baby we left grow so big.'

'I know. You know in your head that she's grown up but your heart still remembers her as she was when you left. I was just as surprised myself.'

'You think we should wake her? If she sleep now, she won't sleep when night come.'

I opened my eyes but it wasn't Aunt Phyllis in front of me. The person in front of me was just like in the photograph, a pretty round face with a pair of deep dark eyes that were looking at me now like she would like to eat me.

'Mama?'

'Me Putus! Me little Pumpkin!'

Her arms opened wide and I flew into them. Mama hugged me so tight that I was gulping for air. I breathed in the sweet smell of her, the smell of flowers and fresh air. And a memory started to wake up in my brain. I remembered this smell from a long time ago. I was laughing and crying at the same time. Mama was crying too. We were so happy and so wrapped up in ourselves, we didn't even see when Cousin Sophie left the room.

Chapter Thirteen

'You granny a'right when you left her?'

'She fine, ma'am. She send a letter and some things for you and Cousin Sophie. They in the suitcase. I will go and ask Cousin Sophie to open the car so I can get them out.'

'No need for that. Sophie bring them in while you sleeping. She put them in your room.'

'Oh, I will go and get them then, if you show me where me room is.'

'You mean to say Sophie don't show you where you sleeping yet? My goodness . . .'

'She fell asleep before I had a chance.' Cousin Sophie was back in the room. She was looking a bit worried and I could see she wanted to say something to Mama because she kept looking at her, but when she saw me looking at her she smiled a little lopsided smile and stretched out her hand to me. 'Come, Joy, I'll show you the rest of the flat and your bedroom.'

It seemed a bit strange to me that Cousin Sophie was offering to show me my bedroom. I thought Mama would want to do that herself. But when I glanced enquiringly at her, she was pouring herself a cup of tea, so I went with Cousin Sophie out of the door. I started to close the door behind me, but Mama was there with her cup of tea in her hand.

'Hold on, sweetheart, I coming with you.'

I was glad. I liked Cousin Sophie, but she was like a stranger to me. Mama was a little like Auntie Phyllis, just a bit plumper and shorter and she laughed a lot more. She was exactly like I always thought she would be. Although not absolutely exactly. Now that she was standing up, I was surprised to see how short she was. She was much shorter than I remembered and Cousin Sophie seemed to tower over her. I guessed I got my height from Papa because I was already nearly as tall as Mama.

Cousin Sophie had a nice flat. I was surprised when I went into her room to see a big photo of me on her dressing table. I was sure it was the one I'd sent to Mama when I started grade six.

'I know that photo,' I said.

'Yes,' Cousin Sophie laughed. 'It was such a nice photo that I thought I would like one as well, so we had a copy made.'

'Oh.'

'Eh, eh. You didn' think I would give away you photo, did you?' Mama tugged playfully at the twist of plaits on my head. 'You have a nice hairstyle, chile. Who do it for you?'

'Cousin Elaine, ma'am,' I said, grateful for the change of subject. I was glad Mama hadn't given away my picture, but guilty that I had thought even for a minute that she would have.

The kitchen was bigger than Granny's front room and I thought Gran would love to have all that space to cook in, especially when all the relations came round. Thinking about Granny wasn't a good idea. I blinked rapidly and concentrated on the door that Cousin Sophie was opening in front of me.

'And this is your room, Joy.'

'My room?' I turned to Mama. 'Why I not staying with you?' I couldn't keep the shake out of my voice, though I really tried.

Mama squeezed my shoulder with her free hand. 'I only have the one bedroom upstairs, sweetheart. Sophie have more space than me so it better for you to stay with her.'

Cousin Sophie winced like she was feeling pain. I wondered what was wrong with her, but Mama drew me into the room.

'So what you think of you new room, eh?'

I looked at the single bed with the frilly bedspread that matched the curtain at the window and the giant teddy bear propped up on the pillow. I let my eyes wander over the dressing table where my backpack sat like it was right at home beside a Barbie doll clock; to the matching chest of drawers and wardrobe. Then I looked down at the thick, pink carpet. My suitcases were in the middle of the floor. My eyes travelled to Cousin Sophie's face. She was looking a little anxious and I suddenly felt like I wanted to give her something to be anxious about. The disappointment of not being able to stay with Mama was making me spiteful.

'I not too particular to pink meself.' I said the words slowly, watching the light leave her eyes. She looked like the bottom had just fallen out of her best pudding pan. It served her right. She knew Mama was sending for me, so why did she have to be so selfish as to take the bigger flat? She must know I would want to stay with Mama.

But I didn't feel so good. I could hear Granny's voice in my head. 'Do unto others as you would that they should do to you.'

It was no good. Even thousands of miles away, Gran was still making sure I acted right. I smiled at Cousin Sophie. 'But this is the nicest pink I ever see. Is a really nice room, Cousin Sophie. Thank you.'

'Are you sure? If you don't like it we can change the colour, you know. What's your favourite colour? We'll go and get some paint tomorrow. It's no problem to change it.'

She was talking fast and she still looked a little anxious, but she didn't look like somebody had just thumped her in the stomach any more.

'Don't put yourself to any trouble on my account. This is fine. I will just get those things Granny send for you.'

I headed for the suitcases, quickly before she could ask me anything else about the room. I wasn't sure how much longer I could pretend.

'You want us to help you unpack, Pumpkin?' Mama had been quiet all the time, just watching me and Cousin Sophie, but now she came over to where I was kneeling by the suitcases. I shook my head. I would really like to be by myself for a little while.

'No, ma'am, I can manage. It won't take long.'

Sophie walked over to the wardrobe and opened the door. 'Well there's plenty of room here to hang your things. I – we've got you some winter things already, but if you don't like them we'll take them back and you can choose what you want.'

I jumped up and hurried over to the wardrobe. I loved the clothes Mama bought and sent to me in Jamaica. The wardrobe was already half full. Jumpers like the one I was wearing, skirts and trousers. Granny had never let me wear trousers because the Church of the Holy Silence didn't believe in women wearing 'men's clothes'. I'd always wished I could wear trousers like Nadine. Now I had six pairs of my own.

I grabbed one off the hanger and held it up against my waist. It looked like it was going to be a perfect fit. I ran to Mama and gave her a big hug.

'Thank you, Mama. They really nice and they going to fit nice too.'

Mama looked a bit uncomfortable. She turned me to Cousin Sophie.

'Is Sophie you have to thank for them, honey. She do all the clothes shopping round here.'

'Oh!' I couldn't keep the surprise out of my voice. 'Thank you, Cousin Sophie.'

'You're welcome. But you don't have to keep saying "Cousin" every time you use my name, you know. Plain Sophie will do.'

She must be mad. How did she expect me to use her first name when she was so much older than me? Granny would tell me off if I even forget to address Cousin Elaine properly, and she was only five years older than me, never mind Cousin Sophie who was a big woman. I looked at Mama expecting her to help me out, but she was just sipping her tea and watching the two of us. She wasn't saying anything. I decided to keep quiet. Maybe if I didn't talk to her unless she was looking straight at me, I wouldn't have to use her name at all. I didn't suppose I would be spending much time with her anyway. I would be with Mama most of the time, for sure.

When she realized that I didn't intend to say anything more, Cousin Sophie sighed and turned to the door.

'I'll leave you to unpack then. Come and join us in the kitchen when you've finished. Supper will be ready. I hope you like spaghetti.'

Luckily for me, she seemed to want to get out of the room fast, so I didn't have to tell her I'd never had spaghetti. I hoped I liked it. I didn't want another business like the one with the tea, especially with Mama watching. I didn't want her to think she had an idiot for a daughter.

I wasn't sure whether or not to unpack the suitcases. I wanted to dilly-dally as long as possible because I didn't feel comfortable in Cousin Sophie's company. But I wanted to hurry so that I could be with Mama. I didn't understand why we couldn't eat just the two of us, the first night we had together.

As soon as I thought that, I felt ashamed. Cousin Sophie had been really good to meet me at the airport, let me stay in her flat and buy me all those nice clothes. I suppose Mama was too busy at work to do the shopping herself, but it was still really kind of Cousin Sophie to help out like that.

I hung up the last dress, closed the suitcases and stood them in the corner. I took up the two parcels and the letters that Granny had sent for Mama and Cousin Sophie and took a deep breath. Then I opened the door and stepped out to face the spaghetti.

Chapter Fourteen

There was a lovely smell coming from the kitchen when I went into the dining room but I hardly noticed. I was too busy admiring the pretty lace table-cloth and the candles floating in the dainty glass bowl of water. Only the wall lights were on, and the dining room looked magical. Mama took the parcels and the letters and put them on the sideboard by the wall.

'I will put these here until after we eat. Come, sweetheart, sit beside me here.'

I sat down in the chair she pulled out for me. I was really hungry because I hadn't eaten that much in the plane. I'd been feeling choked up then from saying goodbye to Gran and Nadine.

Cousin Sophie came in from the kitchen and put a bowl on the table. I lost my appetite straight away. The spaghetti looked like a bowl of tapeworms.

'Now don't feel that you have to eat it all, Joy,' she said, lifting a bundle on to my plate, 'Just have what you can and leave the rest.' She ladled some sauce on top.

Great, I thought. Blood an' worms.

I managed to get the spaghetti into my mouth. It

didn't taste too bad either. It was true that when I went to bite into it my teeth just sank right through and it felt like food for invalids who didn't have any strength in their jawbones, but when I mixed it with the meat sauce it was all right. Not brilliant, but all right. And the garlic bread and salad were lovely.

'That was nice, Cousin Sophie,' I said when I'd finished. 'Thank you very much.'

Sophie smiled, the first time I'd seen her smile without the worried look in her eyes. She took up the napkin beside my plate and held it out to me. 'You might want to use this, Joy. On second thoughts,' she put the napkin down again, 'perhaps you'd better come to the bathroom with me. This is a job for a flannel.'

I didn't always understand when Cousin Sophie talked but I was learning that if I just kept quiet I would figure out what she meant by and by, so I followed her into the bathroom, even though I couldn't understand what I had to do with a piece of flannel cloth. She stopped in front of the mirror over the sink and turned my head.

'Look.'

She was grinning and I couldn't help laughing myself. My mouth was decorated with tomato sauce. I even had some on my forehead and how it got there I didn't know.

'Eh, eh. Look at me face. I look like a fowl just come from mango walk.'

'That's exactly what Granny used to say to me when I was in Jamaica. "Girl, go and wash you face. You look like a fowl just come from mango walk."'

'Gee, Cou – you sound just like Granny. How you do that?'

'What? You mean like, "Eat up that cho-cho, child. Waste not want not."'

It was like Granny was in the bathroom with us.

'Granny used to say that to you too?' I found it strange to think of Granny saying that to Cousin Sophie. I couldn't see her in Granny's house at all.

'Every time she cooked cho-cho and saltfish,' Sophie said. 'I used to pick out the fish and leave the cho-cho on the plate. Couldn't stand it.'

'Me neither. I used to put it in the bin when Granny not looking.'

We were smiling at each other just like Nadine and me when we were sharing a joke that nobody else knew. Maybe it wouldn't be so bad staying with Cousin Sophie for the time being; just until Mama sorted out a bigger place for the two of us to live. I was sure she wouldn't want me to sleep at Cousin Sophie's indefinitely.

Cousin Sophie opened a cupboard behind her.

'Let's get you that flannel.'

She handed me a rag. I waited, but she closed the cupboard door so I figured that she was talking about the rag when she said 'flannel'. It was going to take a long time for me to understand everything in England.

91

When we got back into the dining room Mama had two teapots on the table with three cups and saucers.

'I make the tea while the two of you having your conference. I make some lemon and ginger for Joy. I don't suppose your Granny allow you to drink tea, eh?'

'No, not black tea, Mama, but I like ginger tea and I like lemon leaf tea too.' I remembered just after I said it and I looked at Cousin Sophie expecting her to say something, but she just winked and smiled at me. I grinned. She poured out the tea for Mama from one teapot and then she handed me a cup from the other one.

'There you are, Joy. One horrible tea.' She put one teaspoon of sugar in and stirred it. 'Taste it and tell me if it's OK.'

I took a tiny sip and although it was really hot, it tasted all right to me. Almost as nice as the tea we make from fresh lemon leaf and ginger.

'This taste all right,' I said, surprised. 'Why you call it horrible tea?'

'Horrible tea?' Cousin Sophie looked perplexed like she didn't know what I was talking about. Mama started to laugh.

'Not "horrible tea", Pumpkin. Herbal tea. Mind you, I think your name more spot on. Why anybody would want to drink that when they can get a nice dose o' caffeine is a puzzle to me.'

Oh boy. I'd slipped again. As Granny would say, a whole lot of banana skin 'bout this place.

'Don't worry, me love, you will soon get used to Sophie English accent.'

'I haven't got an English accent.' Cousin Sophie was well put out, but when she saw the look of disbelief on our faces, she looked a little shamefaced. 'Well, not a very strong one. Do I? I mean, you can still tell I'm Jamaican, can't you?'

I kept quiet because I was trying hard not to laugh. I didn't know which Jamaican Cousin Sophie had ever heard talking like that. Apart from Sister Walters, and she was a special case.

'Oh, come on. Unoo just winding me up!'

I had to laugh then. Even when she was talking Jamaican, Cousin Sophie sounded foreign. Mama was laughing too, her eyes twinkling like fireflies on a dark night.

'Give it up, girl. I keep telling you that you is a real Englishwoman now. No matter how hard you try, you can't get away from it.'

'How come you don't have a English accent, Mama? You been here as long as Cou – Sophie.'

'You can't teach old dog new trick, me dear. I been a Jamma woman too long to start being anything else now.'

'And you didn't have people making fun of your accent at college, so you didn't have any reason to change.'

Mama's eyes softened as she looked at Sophie.

'That is true. You did have a hard time, kid. I use

93

to feel guilty dragging you from you nice home to go through that.'

Cousin Sophie shook her head. 'You didn't drag me anywhere. It was my decision to come, so don't blame yourself. And anyway, that experience just toughened me up, so there was no real harm done.'

'Except it turn you into a Englishwoman.'

'Sometimes you get tired of fighting. And then it's easier to fit in.'

I didn't know about that. I was certain I would never let anybody force me to change the way I talked. No way.

'All the same . . .'

I don't know what else Mama was going to say because I heard a ringing from the little table behind me. I jumped like somebody had dropped a pot of hot water in my lap. I couldn't help it. I didn't expect it at all. I was lucky that neither Mama nor Sophie noticed. Sophie was leaping out of her chair and dashing to pick up the phone. She said 'Hello?' in her ordinary voice and then 'Hi' in a voice soft as a blanket. I didn't need Mama's little look to tell me she was talking to someone she liked a lot.

'You want to come upstairs and see the flat, Joy? Bring your tea with you.'

I could tell Mama was just trying to give Cousin Sophie some privacy, but it didn't matter. I was so glad to have her to myself at last. I jumped out of my chair almost as fast as Cousin Sophie when she'd heard the phone. Mama signalled to her that we were going upstairs and she nodded and waved bye to us, a big smile on her face. As I was closing the door behind me I heard her saying, 'Yes, she's here. I can't get used to how much she's grown.' I wondered who she could be talking to.

Mama put her arm round my shoulder as we were going up the stairs.

'Me baby! I can't believe you grow so big.'

'Eh, eh, I not a baby any more, Mama. Granny say me a big woman now.'

'Is that a fact?' Mama laughed, a big, body-shaking laugh that was full of merriment, and a shiver of pleasure went up and down my spine. The stairs weren't all that wide, so I kept bumping into the railing as we were going and I nearly spilled the tea, but I didn't care one little bit. I was just so happy to have Mama's arm round me.

'Well, come in, big woman,' she said, pushing open the door of the flat. We were in a living/dining room painted pale green. A soft carpet of a darker ocean green covered the floor. I loved the room at once. 'And this is where I sleep,' she said, beckoning me into a room painted warm apricot.

Sometimes, if I wasn't feeling well, if I couldn't get to sleep or if there was a big storm, I would go and curl up beside Granny in her bed. She would hold me close until I fell asleep again. I gazed at Mama's double bed and tried to imagine how it would feel to curl up beside her in it. I had to bite my lip hard to keep from crying. I didn't know why I was so tearful all of a sudden. It must be the England air because I don't ever cry. Hardly.

I could see that Mama's flat wasn't as big as Cousin Sophie's and it made sense for me to stay downstairs, but I really wished I could stay upstairs. After seven years apart, it didn't seem right that we should still not be able to be together. Mama must have been thinking the same thing because every two minutes she'd stop the tour, spin me round to face her and say, 'Make me look at you. Me baby! I can't believe it.' All the time she was showing me the flat and talking to me, she was holding on to my hand like she thought I would disappear if she let go. Not that I was complaining.

By the time we got back downstairs I felt like we'd only been apart for a few weeks instead of seven years. I had my mother again and I was the happiest girl in England. I just had to think of a way to convince Mama that I needed to be upstairs with her. I wouldn't mind sleeping on the floor if I could just be near her all the time.

Chapter Fifteen

'Good Morning, Cousin Sophie.'

The words were out of my mouth before I remembered that Cousin Sophie didn't like the Cousin part. I clapped my hand over my mouth too late to stop them.

She laughed, a resigned kind of laugh.

'It's OK, Joy. You can carry on saying Cousin Sophie if you like. I don't mind.'

She frowned at the T-shirt and skirt I was wearing. 'Don't you have anything warmer to wear? What about the trousers and jumpers I got you?'

'Oh, but those too good for yard clothes. I will wear those when I going out.'

I hadn't notice before, but Cousin Sophie had a really happy laugh. It reminded me of the gully in Prospect. It started with a gurgle and then opened out like when the stream tumbled down the cliff in the little waterfall. She got up and took my elbow.

'Come on, I got you those clothes to wear, not just to admire.'

In my bedroom she flung open the wardrobe doors and stood examining the contents for a minute. 'What about these?' She fished out a pair of jeans and a blue fluffy jumper. It was different from the jumper I'd been wearing the day before – soft and gentle against my skin. And warm.

Cousin Sophie held my hand as we went back into the kitchen and I got a cosy feeling all over. I sat in the chair she pulled out for me and watched her flitting round the kitchen like a mother bird, opening cupboards and taking out bowls, cups and saucers and two packs of cereal.

'Now let's see. We've got cornflakes or . . . hmm, bran flakes.' She frowned at the pack of cereal in her hand. 'Not a wildly exciting choice, is it? Would you like some toast?'

I wasn't sure if she was offering the toast instead of, or as well as, the cereal, but I'd have preferred the roast breadfruit she had placed with a knife on a plate on the table. She noticed me looking at it and her forehead creased even more.

'Oh yes. I was wondering what to do with that. I'll ask Aunt Aimee to help me with it when she gets back from work.'

'Mama gone to work already?' I couldn't hide my disappointment.

'She looked in before she went, but she didn't want to wake you.'

Cousin Sophie took up the breadfruit and turned it over like she was trying to work out how it was put together.

'I don't know how we're going to heat this. I'm afraid I haven't got a coal fire to put it on.'

'You don't need a coal fire, Cousin Sophie. You can see Granny roast it already. You just need to fry it in some olive oil now. You want me to show you?'

'Do you know how to do it?'

I didn't answer. I just took up the knife and sliced the breadfruit in two.

'Joy, be careful! That knife is sharp. Why don't we just have some cereal and leave this till later?'

I had to laugh. She must think I was still a baby. 'Is all right. I been cooking since I was seven so I know how to use a knife.'

I peeled the skin off the breadfruit and scooped out the heart. Cousin Sophie was watching me anxiously as I sliced the two halves into little pieces.

'I guess Granny taught you how to cook, uh?'

'Yes, although most of the time I just watch her and pick up how she do things. Gran say everybody should learn how to cook and not have to depend on other people for sustenance.'

'Hmm. That sounds like Gran. She was always trying to get me into the kitchen but I couldn't stand cooking, then. After the gas cylinder leaked one time, Grandpa said he wasn't going to waste money on any more gas, so we had to use the coal pots or wood fire.'

'You joking!'

She shook her head. 'I hated the black hands and streaming eyes from all that smoke, so,' she giggled, remembering, 'I used to sneak off with a library book down to the gully until I knew Granny had finished cooking.' She went over to one of the cupboards and started digging around. 'Still, I wish I'd made more of an effort to learn, but it didn't seem important at the time.'

'Well, Granny always say you never too old to learn, so it not too late for you to start now.'

She straightened and looked at me with raised eyebrows. 'What, are you offering to teach me?'

I shrugged. 'I could show you how to do roast breadfruit.'

She chuckled and returned to rummaging in the cupboard. 'Well, we don't get many breadfruits round these parts, so I don't know how useful that skill would be after today. Oh dear, I don't seem to have any olive oil, only vegetable oil. Seems we'll have to leave it after all.'

'Vegetable oil will do.' I took it from her, poured a little into the frying pan and turned the heat down low. I didn't want the breadfruit to get crisp too quickly. 'What you going to eat it with? You want me to do the fried fish that granny send?'

'That – would – be nice.' Cousin Sophie was dragging out her words and looking like she didn't believe I could really do it.

I poured the semi-skimmed milk on the bammy in the bowl and put it aside to soak. The cassava bread would be plump with the milk in no time. I didn't know how that would taste because Granny only ever used ordinary milk, but I would wait and see. Then I turned to the fried fish that Granny had wrapped so carefully in foil. I put the slices of Scotch bonnet pepper on a saucer to one side. I would use them in the sauce because I didn't think Cousin Sophie would have any fresh pepper about the place.

I was surprised to see that she had the tomatoes, onion and garlic I needed to make the sauce for the fish. I'd half expected her to say she didn't have any of those things. It's true she was out of scallion, fresh thyme and lime, but she had something like scallion that she called spring onion, and she had dried thyme on a shelf with a whole lot of other herbs and spices. The lime juice she had in the bottle I figured would do just as well as fresh lime.

'I'll make some tea, shall I?

'The balls of chocolate in that bag that the bammy was in,' I told her.

'Oh. Why don't I just make some cocoa? It will be quicker than this.' She flicked her head towards the bag like it had something nasty in it.

'It won't take long, at all. Honest. You have a pot I can use?' I asked.

The smell of boiling chocolate was soon filling the whole flat. 'Mmm.' Cousin Sophie sniffed the air. 'This brings back memories.'

I smiled. She wouldn't get that from a tin of cocoa. Even though I say it myself, the breakfast looked scrumptious when I'd finished.

'Joy, this is absolutely delicious,' Cousin Sophie said through a mouthful of breadfruit. 'I could get used to this. I don't remember bammies being so light and puffy when Granny used to cook them.'

A little tingle of pleasure coursed through me. 'It would be nicer if I did use butter instead of vegetable oil to fry them in,' I told her.

She shook her head. 'Don't you know how bad animal fats are for you? And it's lovely as it is.'

'I wish Mama was here to try some,' I said wistfully.

'Why don't you help her to cook hers when she comes home?'

'That's a good idea, Cousin Sophie!'

She smiled her lopsided smile and turned her head towards the window. I followed her gaze. It was not raining any more, but outside it was dark and grey. It felt like dusk instead of ten o'clock in the morning.

'Cousin Sophie?'

'Mmm?'

'What kill the tree them?'

She looked at me, puzzled, then at the tree I was looking at in the garden.

'Oh, they're not dead.' Another gurgling laugh. 'They're just sleeping through the winter. They'll start growing again in spring.'

'Oh. You think it will snow today?' That's the one thing I'd been dying to see in England.

'No.' She chuckled. 'It's not cold enough for snow yet.'

'You joking!'

'Hmn-hmn. It will get a lot colder before it starts snowing. That's why we need to go and get you some more warm clothes. I didn't get any tights or vests.

Thought you might want to choose those yourself. And you'll need some boots.'

'When Mama coming home?'

'Why?'

'Well, I don't have any money to buy all them things.'

'You don't have to worry about that. I'll give you all the money you need.'

'That's really kind of you, Cousin Sophie. But I can't expect you to spend your money on me. Mama will want . . .'

'Joy . . .' she paused.

'What, Cousin Sophie?'

'You mustn't worry about the money.' She sighed. 'It will all be sorted out, OK?'

'OK.'

'I'll clear up while you're getting ready. It's only fair since you did the cooking. Now go, and hurry up.'

I could see it wouldn't do any good to argue with her. It would be nice to get some new clothes, but I wished I was going shopping with Mama instead of Cousin Sophie.

Chapter Sixteen

'Can we wait until Mama come home? I sure she will want to help, Cousin Sophie.'

'She might be too tired. Why don't we just do it together, then we can surprise her.'

Part of me wanted to wait for Mama. It would be so nice to be doing this with her. But another part just wanted to do it now. That part won. I'd never had a Christmas tree before and I was itching to start decorating it. I dug into the box of gold and silver balls, streamers and the string of lights that Cousin Sophie had produced.

She showed me how to tie the decorations on to the branches. The tree smelled strong in my nostrils, green and fresh and woodland-y. It smelled different from the Christmas tree they used to put up in the town centre in Jonesville, though. I don't think it was the same kind of tree.

Granny never had a tree in the house. I don't think anybody in Prospect ever had a tree, but there was always one in Jonesville and every year we would travel the four miles to the town for the tree-lighting ceremony. Nadine and I always held our breath when they pressed the switch and the whole tree blazed into light. Every year the tree seemed to get bigger and more beautiful than the year before. But that tree was like a little lighted matchstick beside the one Cousin Sophie had shown me earlier in London, after we'd finished our shopping.

And now I had my very own tree to decorate. Cousin Sophie had even let me choose it myself. I'd been confused, unsure which to pick from the huge number outside the shop. In the end I'd just closed my eyes and pointed to one. I know it couldn't have been the best of the lot, but Cousin Sophie had just laughed. 'Good choice,' she'd said.

'Ouch!' I stuck my finger into my mouth and scowled at the tree.

'Watch out for the needles.'

She didn't have to tell me. The tree must have thought it was a nurse, the way it was injecting me whenever I tried to tie on a ball. But it was starting to look pretty special already, even though we hadn't even put on the lights yet.

When we'd finished, Cousin Sophie stepped back and nodded towards the socket. 'Do you want to do the honours?'

I plugged in the Christmas tree lights and switched off the overhead light in the living room. It was just too beautiful for words.

I couldn't wait for Mama to come home. I glanced outside. It was dark. Mama must be working nights. I looked at my new watch. I hoped Mama had enough money to pay back Cousin Sophie for all the things she'd bought me. I saw the time. I shook the watch and put it to my ears. It was still ticking, but it couldn't be right.

'Cousin Sophie, what time is it?'

'Four-thirty. Why? Your watch hasn't stopped, has it?'

'But it can't be so early. Is night already!'

She smiled. 'I had the same shock when I first came over. Wait till the summer. It's still light at ten o'clock then.'

I shook my head in wonder. I had so much to tell Nadine and Granny.

I could hardly contain myself when I heard Mama's key turning in the outside door. She was going to be so surprised. I was holding my breath while Cousin Sophie went to open the door. I couldn't wait to see Mama's face when she saw the tree.

'Aimee, come in here a minute. Joy wants to show you something.'

'Is that a fact?'

She came in, the broad smile on her face as usual, and her eyes went straight to the tree. She couldn't miss it because it was the only light in the room.

'Who-oh! Look at this!'

I was giggling like an idiot. She was really surprised. Just as I knew she would be. She walked round and round the tree, admiring it. 'You two been busy, eh.'

'You want to see what else we buy, Mama?'

'You mean there's more? What happen? You all rob a bank or something?'

'Come and look.' I took her hand and started to lead her to my bedroom.

'Would you like a cup of tea? I'll go put the kettle on.'

Mama nodded and smiled at Cousin Sophie. 'Kid, you're a lifesaver.'

The new clothes were still in the shopping bags in my room. I'd been so eager to dress the tree that I hadn't unpacked them. 'You like me new boots?'

She took one of the boots and turned it round. 'Mmm. Stylish! But you can walk in them heels, Pumpkin? They look a bit tall to me.'

'Mama, that not too tall. Is only an inch or so.'

'Inch and a half at least. I not too sure how good this is for you back. I bet you Granny wouldn't allow you to wear anything like this.'

I took the boot from her and put it back with the other one. Granny wouldn't let me wear it because she'd have needed to fly all the way to England to buy it. There wasn't any call for fur-lined boots in Jamaica. But when I had them on, I felt like one of those models in Elaine's magazines. For the first time, I was glad Cousin Sophie had taken me shopping and not Mama. Mama was too old to understand these things.

'Look at me new clothes.'

I spread out the two pairs of jeans, the windbreaker and the denim jacket first. They were my favourite. They and the boots.

'Very nice.'

Next the three pairs of vests with the matching panties that Sophie called knickers, and then the socks. 'And this is me school uniform.'

I hadn't been too impressed when Cousin Sophie showed me what I was going to wear to school. Grey skirt, thick grey tights that looked like they were bound to itch, and a white blouse. For the first time I found myself thinking about my old blue school uniform with affection. But then she'd shown me the red jumper that I would wear over the blouse and I'd felt a little better. And in the winter I'd get to wear trousers so that was all right.

'Sophie really go to town today, boy,' Mama said.

'I hope you don't mind.'

'Mind? Why I should mind, Pumpkin?'

'Well, is your money really, 'cause you will have to pay back Cousin Sophie for me things.'

'That tea must be ready by now,' Mama said. 'Me throat dry as chip. Come on, let we see what Sophie up to.'

Later, when Mama had gone to her flat, Cousin Sophie and I sat in the living room in front of the fire drinking some of the Milo we'd bought in London and watching the lights flickering on the tree.

'You know what, Cousin Sophie?' I said.

'Mmm?' she said dreamily, and you could tell her mind was not in the room.

'If we was in Jamaica now, we would be telling stories. Let we tell story, you and me.'

She looked at me as if I'd asked her to throw herself off the roof. 'I'm sorry, Joy, but I don't know any stories.'

'You couldn't grow up in Jamaica and not know any stories,' I scoffed.

'Well, I did know some. But honestly, I can't remember a single one. You'll have to ask Aunt Aimee if it's stories you're after.'

I sighed. 'OK, I'll tell you one.'

The fire was casting weird patterns on the wall where the light from the floor lamp was faintest. The wind was a mad dog outside, yapping at the windows and gnawing at the roof. A branch from the tree in the garden snapped with a sound like a shot. It was just the right atmosphere for a duppy story, and ghost stories were my favourite.

But halfway through, Sophie was cracking up. This was not the reaction I was expecting. 'No more,' she begged, spluttering Milo everywhere and holding her stomach. 'Please, I can't take any more.'

I had just done my most scary ghost voice and she should have been quaking with fear. I waited in stony silence till she recovered enough to wipe her streaming eyes. 'Right,' I said. 'Forget the duppy story. I'll tell you an Anancy story instead.'

But she didn't enjoy that very much. 'Ooh,' she said when I'd finished. 'That was a bit gory, wasn't it?' Not the response I was looking for, I can tell you. I got up.

'I think I will go write Gran an' Nadine before I go to sleep,' I told her.

'Good idea. I'll say goodnight then. Sleep tight.'

'Night, Cousin Sophie.'

I decided to go up to Mama's flat next time I was in a story-telling mood. She wouldn't have forgotten all her Jamaican background, that's for sure. I felt sorry for any children Cousin Sophie ever had. They were going to miss out on so much.

Chapter Seventeen

It was already after eight when I got up on Sunday morning. I had a quick shower and got dressed in the green dress I liked to wear to church with Granny. It was still one of my favourites and I thought Mama would be pleased when she recognized it. There was no sign of Cousin Sophie.

I went to the kitchen, helped myself to some cornflakes and a hot chocolate. I washed and dried the cup and bowl and Cousin Sophie still hadn't appeared. There was no sound from upstairs either. What if they had gone without me?

I rushed to her room and knocked. There was a groan from inside. Maybe Cousin Sophie wasn't feeling well. I opened the door and peeked in. She was asleep with the duvet tucked round her up to her neck.

'Cousin Sophie, you sick?'

One eyelid opened slowly then snapped back shut. 'What time is it?'

'Is nearly nine o'clock. You not feeling well?'

'Nine o'clock! Joy, it's Sunday!'

Both eyes flew open and a frown creased her

forehead. 'Why are you dressed up like that? Is there a wedding I should know about?'

'Is Sunday, remember? And if you don't hurry, we going to be late.'

'Late?'

'For church.' Where else would we be going on Sunday morning?

'Oh.' She said it like I had suggested we go to the moon.

'You not going to church?'

She pulled herself up, plumped up her pillows and sat back against them. She patted the side of the bed for me to sit down and I perched on the edge. I didn't want to crease up my dress before I'd left the flat.

'Joy, I haven't been to church in – oh, about six years. I went a couple of times after I came here, but . . . well, I didn't think it was for me.

I stared at her. 'You don't go to church?'

She shook her head.

'But . . . but everybody go to church, Cousin Sophie.'

She laughed and shook her head. 'No, Joy, lots of people don't go to church, even in Jamaica.'

'Mama?'

Another shake of the head. I got up slowly and turned towards the door.

'I will leave you to sleep then.'

'Joy.'

I stopped, hopeful.

'If you really want to go, I'll take you next Sunday.'

'Yes, Cousin Sophie.'

I didn't exactly have a burning desire but what made me feel bad was the fact that I'd promised Gran before I left that I would go to church. I'd promised to let her know what I thought about worship in England. I sat on my bed feeling foolish, dressed up like that with nowhere to go. It just didn't feel right to be staying at home on Sunday when I wasn't sick or anything.

'Granny,' I whispered. 'What I must do?'

Cousin Sophie was surprised to see me back so soon.

'I sorry to disturb you again, Cousin Sophie, but if you could tell me where the church is, I will go on me own.'

She looked hard at me. 'You really want to go, don't you?'

I nodded.

'OK, give me five minutes.'

Once we had a visitor in church, someone from America visiting relatives. He came in ordinary corduroy trousers and a shirt open at the neck without a tie or anything. Afterwards at home I'd asked Gran about it.

'Gran, you see what that man wear to church.'

'Hmm hmm.'

'Well, don't you think is a disgrace?'

'Joy, 'member, "man look on the outward appearance but God look on the heart". First Samuel 16, verse 7.'

'In that case we don't really need to dress up for church then.' She gave me a steely-eyed look. 'Suppose the Queen of England should decide to come and visit you. You wouldn't put on you best clothes to go and meet her?'

'But of course, Granny.'

'Well then, every week the King of Heaven and Earth come to meet with you in church. So what kind o' clothes you going put on to meet Him?'

I was silent and she smiled. 'Who know better, do better,' she said.

So perhaps she wouldn't have moved a muscle when Cousin Sophie came out in a pair of casual trousers and the jumper she'd worn to the shops the day before. But when I saw her, my heart sank.

'So you not staying at church with me?'

'Sure I am. Why?'

'Well – nothing, I just thought . . .'

She waited, brows raised questioningly. But I didn't have the courage to tell her that people don't wear their everyday clothes to church. And women certainly wouldn't wear trousers.

'Joy,' she said. 'I think you might find that you don't need to dress up quite so much. Are you sure you want to wear that hat?'

I grabbed hold of my hat in case she decided to take it off. 'Cousin Sophie, you mad? I can't go in God's house with me head uncovered!' She was going to feel so out of place but I wasn't going to say anything else to her. She should know that herself anyway.

Boy, was I in for a surprise.

I could tell the church was old from the way the moss looked at home on the building. It was so big, it made the Holy Silence church building in Prospect look like a rabbit hutch. I hurried in through the door and stopped. One or two people turned round, stared and looked away again. I could tell they were trying hard not to laugh.

I looked at the handful of people in that big old church. They were all as casually dressed as Cousin Sophie and, although I could see a few skirts and jumpers, most of the women wore trousers. I saw myself standing there in my fancy green dress, stockings, patent leather shoes and black hat with my handbag over my shoulder and I could have died.

All through the service I sat with my hands clasped in my lap and when it finished I rushed out before anyone could come and say anything to me. Cousin Sophie had to rush to catch me up.

'Hey, where's the fire?'

I didn't answer her. Nobody was going to catch me going to that church again.

Chapter Eighteen

Granny says 'trouble never set like rain' and now I know that's true. Your whole life could be getting ready to collapse around you and you wouldn't get any warning. When Cousin Sophie called us from downstairs, about noon on Christmas day, I didn't have a clue what was in store for me.

'Coming!' Mama shouted. And we went down hand in hand, laughing at some silly joke which I can't even remember now.

Cousin Sophie was waiting for us at the bottom of the stairs with a big grin on her face. 'Gareth's here.'

I'd been spending every minute I could with Mama. Sometimes I thought Cousin Sophie didn't like the amount of time I spent upstairs in the evenings, but just because she took time off to be with me while Mama was working, it didn't give her the right to all of my time, did it? It wasn't that I didn't like Cousin Sophie or anything, but I still couldn't be natural with her the way I could with Mama. It was the way she talked. I had to strain to understand her sometimes. Mama said it was living in Oxford for three years when she'd first come to England that had done it.

Even now, if I hadn't been hearing his name like a chorus all week, I would be sure she'd said 'Garth' and not 'Gareth'. She led us into the living room where a man was sitting on the sofa with a little boy on his knee. I stopped, startled.

The way Cousin Sophie had been talking about Gareth, I got the impression that she liked him a lot. But I must have made a mistake. This man was white. Maybe it was a different Gareth. But there was his son Daniel that Sophie had been going on about. I wasn't prepared for this.

'Eh-eh, Gareth, I didn't hear your car. How you doing, boy? Merry Christmas.'

'Aimee! It's great to see you.'

He put the little boy on the seat beside him, hurried over, hugged Mama, and kissed her on her cheek. 'Merry Christmas!'

Mama went to sit beside the boy. 'Hello, Daniel, me sweetheart. Aren't you going to give me a kiss today?'

'Hello, Aimee.'

I shook my head. I couldn't be hearing right. I was sure he couldn't be more than three or four but he was calling Mama by her first name! I waited for Mama to teach him some manners, but still smiling, she just bent her head to take his kiss. I was confused, but I didn't have time to try and work out what was going on. The man was talking to me.

'You must be Joy.' He held out his hand. 'I'm Gareth. Gareth Graham.'

I bent my head back and looked up into a pair of bright green eyes. Aunt Phyllis had a cat with green eyes, but I'd never seen anybody with that colour eyes before. It didn't look natural. I felt like those eyes were looking right into my soul and winkling out everything I was thinking. I stuck out my hand.

'Pleased to meet you, Mr Gareth.'

He threw back his head and his laugh rumbled in my ears. I could hear the merriment bursting out from deep inside his belly. He took my hand and I started to worry that I wouldn't see it again. It was completely lost in his large one.

'No, no. We don't stand on ceremony here. Plain old Gareth will do. OK?'

I didn't say anything. I didn't understand how people could do that. I would feel so uncomfortable calling a big man like him by his first name. But it looked like that was quite all right in England. It was weird.

Cousin Sophie took his hand. 'Come and sit down,' she said softly. I felt strange, watching them like that, but it really wasn't any of my business. She sat down on the other side of him. 'Come and meet Daniel, Joy.' I went over, but I pretended I hadn't seen her patting the seat beside her.

We went on a school trip to Negril beach once. As the bus turned a corner, we saw the sea through the trees and we all went 'oooh!' It was as if the July sky had come down and spread itself over the land. I had the same shock now as I held out my hand to Daniel.

His eyes were that same, deep sky-blue, and they were even more shocking against his almost white hair and pale, pale skin. You could see the blood vessels under the skin on his face, it was so thin. I was scared to touch him in case I accidentally broke a vein or something.

The introductions over, I sat on the carpet in front of the fire. It was so good to feel the heat dancing on my cheeks and to see the flames leaping and diving like they were in a gymnastics competition. I was almost in a trance as I watched them.

The big people's voices were droning in the background but they were not making any impression on me because the fire was drawing me into another world. A world where I wasn't feeling unusually shy and out of place. I was seeing all kinds of pictures in the flames and I don't know how long Mama had been calling my name before I heard.

'Eh-eh, child, where you gone?' She turned to Gareth. 'She didn't hear a word you say.'

'Sorry, sir. You talking to me?'

He opened his mouth to say something, then changed his mind, shook his head so that the black hair bounced up and down, and smiled. I have to admit Gareth had a nice smile. He smiled with his whole face, like Mama and Granny. His eyes crinkled at the corners and sparkled and it made you want to smile back at him.

'I was just wondering how you're finding England so far.'

'Well, sir, it cold for true!'

'Oh, you noticed that, did you?' He chuckled. 'Don't worry, it will get better. Winter doesn't last for ever, not even in England. But tell me, what was it like being reunited with your mother? It must have been strange for you.'

'No, sir. It wasn't strange at all. I been thinking 'bout seeing Mama again for a long time.'

'Yes, but it must have been a surprise for you . . .'

Mama jumped up from the sofa. 'Eat first, questions later, Gareth. Come and help me bring the sorrel down, Pumpkin. It's time we all had some of this Christmas dinner you and Sophie been cooking all day.' I jumped up straight away.

It was true that Cousin Sophie and I had been cooking since eight o'clock that morning. When she'd asked me the previous Monday what Granny and I usually had for Christmas dinner, I hadn't expected her to take me all the way to Brixton Market in London to get yam and plantains and stuff. I had been so excited to see all that Jamaican food in England that I'd got slightly carried away. We had bought yams, coconuts, plantains, sorrel, Scotch bonnet peppers and fresh thyme enough to feed an army.

I'd never cooked a turkey before and she hadn't either, so the two of us looked through Cousin Sophie's recipe books and sorted that out together. And for once she'd accepted that I would be OK in the kitchen and didn't tell me to be careful once.

120

'This stuffing is amazing,' Gareth said later as he was tucking into the turkey. 'What's in it?'

'Sweet potato, sausage meat and a few other things. You can thank Joy for that,' Sophie said.

'I didn' have anything to do with it. Is your cookery book the recipe come from,' I told her.

'But who suggested we try it?'

'Well, it's delicious, whoever is responsible.' Gareth's eyes were dancing as he looked from Cousin Sophie to me. Then he bent his head towards Daniel, who had managed to get roast potatoes all over his seat. 'You enjoying that, Dan?'

Daniel nodded. 'Can I have some more bananas?'

We all laughed as Mama put some more plantains on his plate. We must have told him at least three times, but he insisted on calling them bananas. It felt good, like we were all one family. Now that I wasn't receiving all the attention, I could be at ease and join in the conversation without feeling self-conscious. By the time we were having Aunt Phyllis's cake and the drink of sorrel Mama and I had made, I was so relaxed that I was almost asleep.

'Why don't we go and open the presents now?' Sophie suggested when we were all leaning back in our chairs unable to have another bite.

'Yes, yes, presents!' Daniel squealed and we trooped next door to the living room.

Daniel was having a great time bringing the presents from underneath the tree and handing them out, though I had to read the names for him. I hadn't got anything for Gareth and Daniel because I'd only found out the night before that they were coming, so I was a bit embarrassed when Daniel took up two parcels and came smiling towards me. 'I know who these are for,' he said, very pleased with himself.

'So you should,' Gareth said. 'Seeing you chose them.'

I was sitting on the carpet with my head resting against Mama's knee. Cousin Sophie was sitting on the sofa next to her and Gareth was on the other side of Cousin Sophie. After the first two trips to the tree, Daniel got tired of stretching across me and just handed me the presents to hand to their owners.

'This is for you,' he said, holding out one of the parcels. 'And this is for your mum.'

'Thank you, Daniel,' I said, and passed the second parcel to Mama.

Daniel was about to turn back to the tree but he stopped. 'No, that's for your mum.'

'Yeah, this is my mum.' I patted Mama's knee.

'No, she's not your mum, is she, Daddy?' He was laughing as if he thought I was joking.

I heard Sophie suck in her breath. Mama said, 'Oh boy!' And Gareth jumped up and led Daniel back to the tree.

'Let's see what else Santa's brought for you, Dan,' he said loudly.

Chapter Nineteen

Daniel couldn't be right, no way. But something was wrong. Cousin Sophie was concentrating on her hands, clasping and unclasping them in her lap. Mama was looking anxiously at the fire. Neither of them would look at me. There was a sudden, heavy silence in the room.

After a moment, Gareth came to sit beside Cousin Sophie. 'I'm sorry. I forgot about Daniel knowing,' he said.

Mama sighed. 'Is my fault. I was thinking it was best to wait, but now is as good a time as any, I suppose.'

Nobody was talking to me. Nobody was looking at me, or at each other. I swivelled round to look at Mama.

'Mama?'

She put her hand on my head. It felt like a basket of bricks.

'Sweetheart, we have something to tell you.' She stopped. I waited. Cousin Sophie took my hand in hers. Mama started speaking again. 'I want you to know that I love you very much. I will always love you, no matter what. You going always be me own little Pumpkin. You believe that, don't you sweetheart?'

I nodded. There was a ball of dread rising like dough in my stomach. My heart was threatening to burst through my chest. I couldn't bear the suspense any longer. 'Mama, what you trying to tell me?'

'Pumpkin.' She sighed. 'This is so hard. What we trying to say is that you mother . . . that I am . . . I am not your mother.'

I felt like somebody was holding my heart and squeezing. All the blood was rushing to my brain. I was going to faint.

'Joy?' Cousin Sophie's voice seemed to come from a long way away. 'Are you all right?'

The floor tilted back to its right place and my head cleared.

'You joking, right, Mama?' I tried to laugh, willing them to laugh with me, prove it was just a joke.

Silence.

'You not me mother?'

'I'm sorry, Joy. We didn't want to tell you like this. We were going to wait until . . .'

'You really not me mother?' I wasn't even listening to Cousin Sophie. This didn't have anything to do with her. I was just staring at Mama, trying to force her to tell me it wasn't true.

'Sweetheart, I was only keeping you until you real mother could look after you and,' her voice shook, 'I have to give you back to her now.'

'So who is me mother?' My voice was small and timid. I knew of course, I'm not that stupid. But I had to hear it from Mama for myself. She knew that I knew and she remained silent.

'Cousin Sophie?'

She nodded.

I don't believe you. I don't believe you. I don't believe you. I don . . . I was chanting it over and over in my head. I hoped if I said it enough times it wouldn't be true. I didn't realize I was saying it aloud until Cousin Sophie reached out to squeeze my shoulder.

'It's going to be all right, Joy. It's . . .'

I shook off her hand and clutched at Mama's knee.

'Mama, please say is not true,' I begged.

'Sweetheart, I wish I could. I would give anything in the world to be your mum. But things didn't work out that way.'

I let go of her knee then, wrapping my arms round my chest, rocking back and forth on the floor. I was trying to keep the pain inside.

'You been lying to me all these years.' It was just a whisper, but they heard.

'Sweetheart, don't say that.'

I turned fiercely on Cousin Sophie. 'Well, what else you call it?'

'Joy, perhaps if . . .'

'I sorry, but I wasn't talking to you, Mr Gareth.'

'Joy!'

For a minute I thought Granny was in the room

and her wrath was going to fall on my head, but her voice was only in my mind. It had just merged with Mama's shocked tone.

'Aimee, it's all right. She's just had a shock.'

'That's no reason for her to forget herself . . .'

I didn't hear the rest. That was the final straw. It was the first time Mama had told me off for anything. I rushed out of the room before the threatening tears could complete my humiliation.

I flung myself on my bed and waited for the eye-water to start flowing, but not a drop came. My eyes were burning and my throat was tight and itchy like sandpaper. I knew that the tears would ease the burning sensation, but I couldn't cry. I wanted to be in my old room in Jamaica again with Granny snoring next door. I wanted Granny so badly that it was a pain inside my chest, making my breath come out in short gasps. And then I remembered. She was not my granny.

Chapter Twenty

I heard Gareth's car leaving and then the door slam. I guessed that was Mama going upstairs. Good. I didn't want to see her ever again. Later I heard Sophie's knock on the door.

'Joy? Are you awake?'

I lay in the dark, listening to the raindrops tapping on the window and the swish of the car tyres on the road outside. I willed her to go away and eventually she went. I lay like that trying to think, but only one thought kept going round my head. Mama was not my mother.

But it wasn't just that Mama wasn't who I always thought she was. Papa was not my father either, Gran was not my grandmother, Aunt Phyllis and Uncle Bob were not my aunt and uncle, and Elaine was not my first cousin. I was not me.

Joyanna Patterson was someone they had made up. But who was this person in her place? Who was I? If Sophie was my real mother, who was my father? And what was my real name? What was I going to call everyone?

I couldn't go on calling Sophie 'Cousin Sophie', but

127

I couldn't bring myself to address her as plain 'Sophie' and calling her 'Mama' was out of the question. What was I going to call Mama? Why did I have to be thousands of miles away from Gran just when I needed her most? Why hadn't Gran told me? How could she have let me come here to face this on my own? It was a long time before I finally fell asleep.

I was intending to stay in my room all day but by eleven o'clock the next morning my tummy was rumbling like thunder. I didn't think I was going to last the day. And I desperately needed to use the bathroom.

When I came out, she was standing in my doorway waiting for me.

'Joy, we have to talk,' she said. 'Can I come in?'

I shrugged. 'It's your flat, I can't stop you.' I nearly added 'Cousin Sophie' but stopped myself in time. It would be silly to keep calling her that, when she wasn't my cousin. I slumped on to the bed and she came and sat beside me. I shuffled up, away from her and she flinched.

'Joy, I know it's hard for you . . .'

Oh really? How could she know what I was feeling? She had not just been told she had been living her whole life as someone else.

'I was very young when you were born,' Sophie said. Well I didn't need her to tell me that. I could have worked it out for myself.

'Grandpa went ballistic when he found out. Said I wasn't to bring *it* into his house. He wanted me to

128

give you away. Said I couldn't stay in the house if I kept you.' She looked at me then and her eyes went even darker, remembering. I felt a bit strange, but I folded my arms more firmly across my chest. In my book there was just no excuse for abandoning your child.

'So you did what Grandpa wanted,' I said bitterly. 'Thanks, *ma'am*!' I put as much sarcasm as I could into the last word and was glad to see that the message got through. 'Some mother,' I sneered. 'I hope you're not waiting for me to call you Mama because you'll have a very long wait.'

'Course not,' she said, her voice low. 'Anyway, people don't say "Mama" in England. They say "Mum".'

'I'm not calling you that either,' I said fiercely.

'I'm not asking you to. Honestly, Joy, if you'd just—'

'Good,' I interrupted. ''Cause I won't. You might have given birth to me but, as far as I'm concerned, you're not my mother. Mothers don't give away their children.'

She turned her head away. 'You don't understand, Joy. I'm trying to tell you—'

'I understand all right,' I interrupted. 'I understand you didn't want me. You know how that makes me feel?'

'Would you just listen to me for a minute?'

Good. She was getting rattled. I didn't let up. 'I'm not staying here with you,' I said fiercely. 'I'm going back to Granny. She's a better mother than you will ever be.'

She sighed. 'You're upset now. We'll talk later, when you're ready.'

And I never will be, I thought. She went out, closing the door quietly behind her. I flopped back on to the bed. I felt awful. First hot, my skin dry as a desert, then cold as an icicle. I wanted Mama to come and say it was all a mistake, nothing had changed and I was still her daughter. I wanted everything to be the way it was. I wanted Gran. I wanted to be back in Jamaica. And I wanted to be as far away as possible from the two people who'd betrayed me.

Chapter Twenty-One

I stayed in my room until early afternoon when hunger forced me into the kitchen. Sophie was sitting at the table with a pile of papers in front of her but she was not doing any work. Instead she was staring through the window like a zombie. She jumped up when she saw me.

'Joy! There you are. Would you like something to eat?'

I didn't really want to talk to her, but there was a big old worm gnawing at my insides. And besides, I thought that I would need to build up my strength if I was to plan my escape from these two. I nodded.

She sat watching me while I ate the chicken sandwich she'd made. I felt like a fly in a spiderweb and ate as fast as I could. I couldn't wait to get back to my room but, as soon as I'd swallowed the last bite, she pounced.

'Would you like to talk now?'

'No, thank you.' The last thing I wanted was a cosy little heart-to-heart chat with her.

'Don't you have any questions you want to ask me?'

I shrugged. 'No.' It wasn't true. I had a million

questions I wanted to ask her, but I wasn't sure I wanted to hear the answers. And how would I know she would tell me the truth this time? Lying can become a habit. Anyway, I had to try to answer some questions of my own.

Like, how could I have been so stupid? It was plain as white rice to me now, so how come I hadn't seen it before? Sophie sending my ticket; meeting me at the airport; taking time off work to be with me; buying my clothes; having a room for me in her flat. Any idiot would have known that you don't do all that for someone else's child. It needed a special kind of stupidity to be so blind.

I escaped to my room as soon as I'd washed and dried my plate. Sophie looked up as I was heading for the door.

'Joy . . .'

'I'm going to write to Gran and Nadine,' I said.

'I thought you wrote to them last week?' She frowned.

'I going write them again, to tell them I coming home,' I said and left, closing the door behind me.

I did try to write, but didn't get further than 'Dear Gran'. I couldn't put what I was feeling into words. I couldn't ask the questions I wanted to ask her in a letter.

I spent the rest of the afternoon looking through the scrapbook 6A had made for me. I looked at all the faces, tracing their outlines, reading what they had written and remembering. I stared longest at Nadine. I stared so hard that my eyes began to water. I snapped the book shut and lay on my bed, gazing blindly at the ceiling.

By six o'clock I was sick of my own company and hungry again. There was no one in the kitchen, but I could hear voices coming from the living room, and thought Sophie must be watching television. I pushed open the door and stopped.

'Come in, Joy,' Mama said. 'We just call your name.'

'We thought you were asleep,' Sophie cut in. 'Would you like a drink?'

'Yes, I'll go and make it.'

I was glad for the excuse to get away, but Sophie got up and took up the teapot, which was on the table beside her. 'No, you sit down. I'm going to top this up anyway. You must be hungry. As soon as Gareth comes, you can have something to eat with Daniel.'

Gareth! I'd forgotten he and Sophie were going to a party in London. So that was why Mama was here. She was on babysitting duty. I bit my lip. I wasn't looking forward to seeing them so soon again after yesterday.

Instead of sitting down, I went to stand by the French windows, and look out at the garden. There was nothing to see, of course, except the dark and the occasional splash of drizzle on the glass. But anything, even the boring blackness outside, was better than the uncomfortable silence in the room.

'I never see so much rain, even for winter.'

I jumped. I hadn't heard her move, but she was right behind me. Her arm was round my shoulder and naturally I leaned back and rested against her. It was what I had done since I arrived and for a moment I forgot everything except how good it was to be with her.

'Me little Pumpkin,' she murmured, and that brought me back to my senses. I was not *her* little anything. Yesterday she was my mother, but today she was not even a blood relation. I pulled away and went to stand by the fire, away from her.

'Please don't call me that.'

'Joy, I know you must feel a little confused now, but is not anything that we can't work out together, sweetheart. I still feel like you mother.'

'But you not, are you?' Even now there was a faint hope that hadn't quite died, but she shook head sadly.

'But that don't mean I love you any less. You know if I had me own daughter I would want her to be just like you. And you will always feel like me own child. I can't help that.'

'But why you didn't tell me before? Why you have to lie to me all these years?' That was what really hurt. That Mama and Sophie could let me believe I was someone that I wasn't. Let me have a life as this

134

someone for eleven years and then just take it away, without even 'excuse me'.

'We wanted to wait until you could understand everything,' Sophie said, coming back into the room. She put the teapot on the table and handed me a cup of Milo. 'Then this opportunity came for us to come to England and we had to leave you with Granny until we could get settled.'

Mama crossed the room to sit on the sofa and retrieved her cup of tea from the floor where she'd left it. 'We couldn't just write you a letter so we decide to wait until you could come over.'

'So why you didn't take me over before? Why you have to wait so long?'

'You was doing so well in school, sweetheart. We didn't want to interrupt you education.'

'Some of our friends in London were sending their kids *back* to Jamaica to school, and you were already there,' Sophie joined in. 'It seemed a shame not to let you finish primary school before up-rooting you.'

Their answers were so smooth, I was sure they had practised. I didn't trust them one bit. Why hadn't Granny told me? Unless they'd told her not to.

Sophie must have read my mind. She leaned over to check the pot of tea and offered Mama some more. Then she poured herself another cup and leaned back in the chair, gazing into the cup as if she would see the words she wanted to say in it. The steam from the cup coated her face with moisture so that she looked as though she was sweating.

'When we decided to send for you, we asked Granny to tell you about your – about me being your mother. I guess she thought it was our job. I expected you to know . . .'

'Oh!' I clapped my hand over my mouth, remembering. 'That's what she was trying to tell me the day before I leave. But Cousin Elaine did come to plait me hair, and then I suppose Granny just forget.'

'What me tell you?' Mama turned to Sophie. 'I know it have to be something like that for you granny not to tell her.'

'So if you did want me to finish primary school, why you send for me now?'

There was silence. I saw Sophie look at Mama and if I hadn't been watching so carefully I would have missed the small shake of Mama's head. I put my empty cup on the table and waited.

'I just couldn't wait any longer to have you with me,' Sophie said, and a blind man could have seen that she was lying. 'I'd been without my baby too long.' I was right not to trust them. I didn't know what they were planning, but they were definitely up to something. Only I wasn't going to stay around to find out what it was.

'Well, I not a baby any more,' I said. 'And I can't call both o' you Mama, so to make things simpler for everybody, I think I better go back to Jamaica.'

'Joy!' Sophie got up to follow me as I headed for the door.

'Leave her. Give her time,' I heard Mama say as I closed the door behind me. I didn't hear anything else because the doorbell went. I continued to my room. I wasn't feeling very much like company.

Chapter Twenty-Two

I liked her straight away. Her brown hair was tied back with a sky-blue scarf, which matched the trouser suit she was wearing. Her grey eyes were calm and kind, and the butterflies in my stomach settled down as soon as she said, 'Hello, Joyanna. Do you want to be called, Joy, Joyanna or Anna?'

'Joy, please, Miss.' Almost immediately I thought I should have said Anna, because I didn't feel like Joy any more. But on second thoughts since I wouldn't be here long anyway, it didn't matter what anyone called me.

'Well, Joy, welcome to Maple Thorpe School. Why don't you sit at this table.' She led me to a long table with six chairs round it. She pulled out a drawer.

'Here, put your pencil case in here and I'll show you where to hang your coat.' She stood watching me as I took my pencil case from my bag and put it in the drawer.

'That's a lovely hairstyle you've got there,' she said. 'How long did it take to do?'

'About an hour,' I told her. A warm glow spread all over me. I'd thought about taking my cornrows out and now I was glad I'd decided to leave them in for a little longer.

I could listen to her voice all day. It was warm and husky and I couldn't imagine her shouting at anyone ever. She sure was different from Miss Jones. Not that Miss Jones was all bad, mind you. She didn't use the strap too much – not like some of the other teachers at Prospect School. But she did like to shout.

By the time Mrs Dean had shown me the girls' toilets and cloakroom it was time for registration. The bell rang just as we got back to the classroom.

'You sit here, Joy,' she said. 'I'll just go and bring the rest of the class.' Her smile was like the sunshine after a shower in the rainy season.

'OK, class, settle down,' Mrs Dean said. And the scraping of the chairs and the slamming of the desks stopped almost immediately. 'Six D, we've got a new member in our class today. This is Joyanna Patterson but she'd like us to call her Joy. Joy's new to England as well as to Maple Thorpe. Would anyone like to guess where she's from?'

A forest of hands went up.

'OK, David?'

A boy with orange hair and a sprinkling of freckles on his snub nose put his hand down. 'Miss, is it America?' he asked.

Mrs Dean turned to me, eyes twinkling as if we were sharing a joke. 'Is it, Joy?' She knew very well it wasn't.

'No, Miss,' I said.

She asked a couple of other children. One guessed Australia and the other France. Each time Mrs Dean asked me if they were right and now it was a guessing game between me and the rest of the class. I wasn't feeling so nervous any more.

'I think you'll have to give us a clue, Joy,' she said when it was clear no one was going to get it.

'Well,' I said, 'it's an island in the Caribbean.'

Straight away more hands shot up. The teacher called on a boy who'd been waving his hand frantically in the air for some time. His black hair was cut very close at the sides, but flopped forward to just above his eyebrows. It made him look very mischievous.

'Alan?'

'Is it Barbados?' he asked.

I grinned. 'You gettin' warm.' He grinned back, his dark eyes warm and friendly.

There was a snigger from a table to the right. Mrs Dean spun round, her face stern. 'Alice?'

Alice had a mass of bright red hair, which made her look like her head was on fire, and freckles all over her face, like a ripe lacatan banana.

'Miss, is she from Africa?'

I couldn't believe it! Everybody knows Africa is a continent, not a country – and Africa in the Caribbean? Half the class was laughing and I joined in. I guessed Alice was not very bright. Mrs Dean pointed to a girl at the back of the class.

'Melanie, would you like to have a guess?'

I'd noticed her before. She hadn't put her hand up once. She was just staring at me, looking like a yellow-headed owl with her short blonde hair and big round glasses. I wondered why Mrs Dean asked her. I was sure if she'd had any idea, she'd have put up her hand.

'Jamaica,' she said. It wasn't a question, just a quiet, matter-of-fact statement. Goes to show, you shouldn't judge people. Melanie was obviously much smarter than she appeared.

It was break and I was sort of shuffling around the playground by myself. I didn't know anybody and it didn't look like anybody wanted to know me. It was freezing, but the sun was shining for a change. Not that it had any heat, but at least the place didn't look so gloomy.

'Hello, Joyanna.'

I turned round. Alice was standing with her arm through another girl's. Her grey eyes were wide and her smile broad. I gave her a big grin, relieved that I wasn't going to have to spend the whole break on my own. She hadn't seemed that friendly in class, but perhaps I'd made a mistake.

'Hi,' I said warmly. She nudged the girl beside her and grinned.

'Ha-eye,' she mimicked me, exaggerating my accent, and they both doubled over, laughing.

They left. I looked around the playground. There were girls skipping, boys were playing football, some of the little ones were playing tag and a group of girls were twirling hula hoops under a large tree. I shuffled over to the side of the building and leaned against the wall. My heart was beating painfully fast and each breath was an effort. The sun wasn't having any effect on the frost, which carpeted the ground and coated the leafless branches of the tree. The cold seeped through my thick duffle coat, scarf and gloves. But the cold inside me was worse. I dug my hand into my pocket and pulled out the purse Sophie had given me. I opened it. It was all there, the five pounds for this week's pocket money and the two pounds for lunch.

I did some quick calculations in my head. About a month, I thought. I didn't know how much a plane ticket to Jamaica would cost, but probably two months at the most would do it. I could last till then.

Chapter Twenty-Three

One day Mrs Dean asked me to collect the exercise books. 'And mind you collect them all,' she said. I looked at her puzzled. Why didn't she want them all? And which ones should I leave? But she was telling the class to line up by the door and I decided to use my initiative. I knew which was the first one I was going to leave. In fact, I decided I wouldn't go near that table. I collected the rest, put them on Mrs Dean's table and went out into the playground.

It was silent reading first thing when we came back in. I loved this part of the day. Fancy having a special time just to read! Mrs Dean was marking the history books. 'Joy?,' she said. 'There seem to be some books missing. Are you sure you collected them all?'

'No, Miss,' I frowned.

'Miss, she hasn't taken mine,' Karen squealed.

'Or mine.' This was Alice. 'Miss she hasn't taken any from this table.'

Mrs Dean was the one frowning now. 'Why didn't you collect those books, Joy?'

'Miss, you told me not to take up all of them.'

She frowned. 'I don't remember saying that.'

I couldn't believe it. I'm not stupid and I know she told me not to collect all of the books.

'Miss, I heard you tell her to make sure she collected all the books. But she doesn't understand English, Miss.'

'Thank you, Alice.' Her voice was sharp, but it didn't make me feel any better. It hurt to find out that Mrs Dean was the same as the other adults in my life. I shouldn't have been so eager to like her. They always let you down in the end.

That day the heating packed up and we were sent home early. I was still smarting from Mrs Dean's betrayal and when I got to the flat I was in a bad mood. I went straight to my room, pushed the door open and froze. Sophie was standing near my bed, one of my jumpers in her hand. She was holding it against her cheek with a strange half-sad, half-happy expression on her face.

She jumped when she saw me and we stared at each other in silence for a minute. 'Joy!' she said. 'I didn't expect you home so early.'

Well, that was obvious.

'The boiler broke. You think I could have some privacy in this place?' I stood by the door, waiting for her to leave.

'I came to see if you had anything for the washing machine. I'm just about to put a wash on,' she said defensively.

'Oh.' She seemed to be waiting for me to say something else. When I didn't, her shoulders slumped and she dropped the jumper back on the chair where I'd left it. 'I'd better go and start supper now you're here.'

There was a knock on the door. I hissed my teeth. What did she want now? Sophie was holding out three letters.

'I almost forgot. These came for you.'

She almost forgot! I grabbed the airmail envelopes. 'Thanks,' I said breathlessly and darted over to my bed, closing the door behind me.

One of the letters was from Granny, the other two from Nadine. I opened Nadine's first. I wanted to savour the anticipation of reading Gran's.

Dear Joy,

I thought you say you would write. Seems the cold freeze off you finger them so you can't hold pen no more. I got your address from Elaine and I just thought I would say hello. How you liking England? You see the Queen yet?

Everything is the same here as usual. Papa give away all of Bessie puppies, but he let me keep the little one you like to remember you. Elsa getting big you see. She trying to sit up now and Mam say she look like she will be crawling soon. I see you granny in the market yesterday and she say you tangerine tree loaded and me and the boys must come and pick them. I like you gran. I think she missing you though. I miss you too girl. Herma want me and she to be friend but she could o' never be me best friend. That will always be you.

Write soon, you hear.

Your bestest friend,

Nadine

Dear Joy,

I just post a letter to you this morning and this evening I get yours. I going to post this now, so if you get them same time, make sure you read the other one first.

So you enjoying yourself in England, girl. London sound nice for true. Me jealous of all them new clothes you buy, you see. You mother must be really rich. You Cousin Sophie sound like she is a nice person so I sure you will get used to her soon. Fancy you seeing Buckingham Palace and everything. I was only joking when I say that bout the Queen, but I didn't know you could just walk up and look at her house like that.

Yesterday I go down to the gully and guess what? You know that mango tree you always say your navel string bury underneath? Well, it have two mangos on it. I never see mango in Prospect this time of year. Mama say is a good sign. It mean you going be happy in England, probly. I watching them till they ripe and then I going eat one for you.

I was buying ice cream today and Maas Josh ask after you. He say to tell you hello for him. Mam and Papa say hi too and the boys say to tell you they miss you stories.

It so hot out here, child, I can't believe what you telling me bout ice on the ground. You sure you not just making fun of me? This is the longest letter I ever write in my whole life, so I going to stop now, but make sure you write back soon. I miss you.

Your bestest friend,

Nadine

147

My dear Joy,

I was very glad to get your letter. Praise the Lord that you reach safely and find the others safe and well. I glad to see that you enjoying the sights in London.

I wanted to write before, but the blood pressure been acting up again. I had to go to the doctor and you would be surprised to see the whole heap of pills I had to take, but I feeling much better now, thank the Lord.

Yes we had a nice Christmas, thank you for asking. Elaine and them come over and we spend the day together, but we all miss you. I hope you had a good Christmas yourself.

Elaine come over to tie out the goat in the mornings and sometimes she stay over at night, especially if the blood pressure acting up. Other than that, everything is much the same as you leave it.

I know there is something else I want to say to you, but I can't remember what it is. The old brain is not

what it use to be. I will most likely remember by the
time I next write, but Phyllis waiting to take this to
the Post Office, so I will end now.

Keep sweet, me darling,

Yours truly,

Granny

Chapter Twenty-Four

I was undoing my cornrows in my bedroom when I heard her knock on the door. I paused with the comb raised above my head in one hand and the end of a cornrow in the other.

'Come in.' I was surprised to see her. We generally met in neutral territory like the kitchen, the dining room or living room these days.

'Here, let me do that.'

I let her take the comb from me and sat on the bed while she undid the plaits.

'Would you like me to cornrow it again?'

'OK,' I said. 'But I have to wash it first.'

'Joy, can I ask you a big favour?' She looked anxious, as if my answer meant a lot to her.

'What?'

'You know Gareth works in London?'

I nodded. He was head of some accounting firm. That's how they'd met. They were at an accounting conference together in Manchester.

'Well, something's come up and he has to go in to work early tomorrow. Too early to take Daniel to the nursery. I was wondering, if you wouldn't mind, seeing that you have to pass that way on your way to school . . .'

'You want me to take Daniel to the nursery?' Why couldn't she just say it?

'We'd also need you to collect him and bring him here on your way home. If you feel you can't, just say so. I'll do it if you can't, of course, but I just thought since you have to go past on your way to school any-way . . .'

'I don't mind.' She looked like someone had just given her a Christmas present. Little did she know I wasn't doing it for them. I was doing it for me because I liked Daniel. I liked listening to him chattering away in his high-pitched voice. I liked to feel his little hand in mine. I even liked it when he planted a big, wet slobbery kiss on my cheek. It almost made up for not being able to play with Nadine's sister.

I was beginning to think Gareth had changed his mind. If they didn't come soon, I was going to be late for school.

'You think him still want me to take Daniel to nursery?' I asked Sophie.

She glanced at her watch and frowned. 'It is getting late, isn't it. Perhaps I should call to make sure every-thing's OK.' She was dialling the number when I heard the car in the drive.

Gareth was looking harassed when Sophie let him in. 'Sorry we're so late. He was a bit fractious and clingy this morning. I couldn't get him to eat his breakfast.' He shot a worried glance at Daniel who was still clinging to his trouser leg as if his life depended on not letting go of his dad. 'I hope he's not coming down with anything.'

It took us a while to detach Daniel from Gareth and by then I was almost late. I thought he was probably tired. Gareth said neither of them had slept well the night before. I had to carry him part of the way and he was tearful when I turned to leave. It was hard leaving him like that, but it was getting late so I didn't have time to reassure him.

When I went to the nursery to collect him later that evening, I couldn't see Daniel anywhere. One of the nursery helpers came up to me.

'Can I help you?'

'I came to collect Daniel,' I said.

'Daniel?'

'Daniel Graham.'

'Oh, have you got a letter?'

'Letter?'

'A letter from his parents to say you can take him?'

'No, but his father said he was going to phone you to let you know I was coming.'

'Just a minute.' She turned to go into the little room at the back, and then she stopped. 'What's your name?'

I told her.

I heard her talking to someone and then she came back.

'Daniel's in the playroom. Just through there. He seemed a bit tired today. Perhaps you should let him have a little nap when he gets home.'

I didn't see him straight away. There were kids everywhere, running around, sliding and swinging. And then I spotted him. He was sitting in the corner of the sandpit, slowly digging his fingers into the sand. He looked sort of listless.

He glanced up when I called his name, lumbered up like an old man and shuffled over to me. He looked a bit red and I felt his forehead. It was warm, but I couldn't be sure if he had a fever or was just hot from playing in the sand. Sophie would know.

When we got home there was a note from Sophie on the kitchen table. *Just gone to the corner shop. Won't be long.*

Great, I thought. Typical of her to be out just when she was needed.

Daniel complained that he was thirsty. I gave him a glass of orange juice, which he drank without pausing for breath. Straight away he asked for another. He finished that as well and held out his glass for more.

'That's enough now, Daniel,' I said. 'You have to leave room for your supper.'

'Don't want any supper.' He put the glass on the table and went to curl up in the chair by the window. Then he rested his head on the arm of the chair and looked like he was about to fall asleep right there.

'Come, Daniel.' I took his hand. 'Come and lie

down on the bed. You can have a little sleep until your daddy comes. OK?'

He was nodding as if his head was too big for his neck. I started to pray that Sophie would come home soon because I had no idea what was wrong with him and I didn't know what I would do if he got worse. I felt his forehead. It was definitely hot.

I thought back to Prospect. When I had a fever once, I remember Granny making a bath of fever grass and bathing me in it. Then she rubbed me all over with bay rum. It stopped the fever in no time. But there wasn't any fever grass in the whole of England and I would bet anything that Sophie didn't have any bay rum anywhere in the flat.

I got a rag – a flannel – from the bathroom, wiped his hands and face and took him into the spare bedroom. I tucked him under the duvet and sat on the edge of the bed.

'Joy.' Poor Daniel. His voice was barely louder than a whisper. You could tell he was feeling sorry for himself.

'Yes, Daniel?'

'Will you read me a story?'

'A story?'

'Daddy reads me a story when I go to bed.'

'Oh. OK . . .' I was pretty sure there weren't any books in the flat suitable for a three-year-old. 'I don't think we have any books you'd like, Daniel,' I said. 'But I could tell you a story instead. Would that do?'

He nodded and I rubbed my hands in anticipation.

I might not be much of a nurse but even if I say so myself, I'm not a bad story-teller, in spite of Sophie's reaction. So a story session with Daniel was very welcome. I was sure he would be a better audience than Sophie. He wouldn't find my duppy voice funny.

'Let me see now. Which one shall I tell you?' I searched my brain for one that I thought he would like. I thought that, being a boy, he would enjoy one with a lot of action. That's the kind of story Nadine's little brothers always asked for.

'All right, Daniel,' I said. 'I'm going to tell you a story about Brer Anancy and Brer Bull.'

'What's a burr?' he asked.

'Not "a brer", just "brer",' I explained. '"Brer" means "brother". So this is a story about Brother Anancy and Brother Bull.'

'Once upon a time,' I started, 'Brer Anancy and Brer Bull were—'

'What's a nan see?' he interrupted.

I could see this story-telling session was not going to be as easy as I thought. 'Anancy is a spiderman,' I told him. 'He's a man who sometimes changes into a spider.'

'I don't like spiders, Joy.'

Oh, boy. I never had this problem back home. I explained that Anancy was a good spider, not the nasty kind, and he agreed that I could carry on with the story. It was the longest story I have ever told, believe me. Every minute Daniel would interrupt.

'What's a dry tree? What's banana trash? Rivers

155

don't have beds, Joy! What's a mango?' I mean, don't they teach them anything in nursery school? And then just when I got to the exciting bit where Brer Bull was ramming the tree with Anancy clinging to the tiny branch at the top, he started snoring. Another first. Nobody had ever fallen asleep in the middle of one of my stories before.

I leaned over and felt his forehead. It was hot for certain. It was then I noticed a bright red spot on his cheek just underneath his left eye. It looked like he'd been stung by an insect. Perhaps that was it. I remembered a story I read about an explorer who was bitten by a poisonous spider in the Amazon jungle. He developed a raging fever and died a slow and very painful death.

I felt Daniel again. Yes, I'd say he had a fever for sure. What if he went to sleep and didn't wake up? Perhaps I should've kept him awake. I shook him gently. He whimpered, but didn't wake up. Did they have poisonous spiders in England? I wouldn't be at all surprised if they did. I tried to think what was good for tarantula bites. Perhaps it had been lurking in the sandpit just waiting for an innocent child to come along so it could take a big bite out of him.

No wonder Daniel didn't like spiders. And there I was telling him a story about a spiderman!

'Daniel,' I whispered.

Nothing.

I reached out to shake him harder. That's when I heard Sophie's key in the door. I dashed out of the room and almost threw my arms round her, but I controlled myself, just in time. Even so, you could tell by her broad smile she was pleased by the welcome.

'Sophie! I so glad you come.'

'Oh? What have you done?' But she was still smiling. I wondered if she would still be smiling when she saw Daniel. I didn't know what I'd done. I suddenly thought of something else. Should you give orange juice to someone suffering from a poisonous spider's bite?

'Is something wrong with Daniel?'

'Well, I'm not sure. He was a bit tearful when I collected him from the nursery. I think you'd better come and look at him.'

There was a high-pitched wail from the bedroom and we both dashed towards the sound. Daniel was sitting up in bed scratching his face and sobbing like tears were going out of fashion and he didn't want to be left with any.

'Oh, sweetheart. What's the matter?'

Sophie took him on to her lap and started rocking him. She reached for a tissue from the box on the bedside table and wiped his tears. 'Tell Sophie what's wrong.'

'There are pictures in my pillow,' Daniel said between hiccups.

'Pictures?' Sophie took the pillow and turned it over. 'There are no pictures there, sweetheart.'

'There are pictures when I sleep.' He was scratching his face and neck all the time he was talking. Sophie held his hand and peered into his face, frowning.

There were at least three spots on his face now. The poison must be spreading.

'What kind of pictures, Pumpkin?'

I bit my lip until I was sure there would be little half moons in my skin. Pumpkin was my pet name. The one Mama had made for me. She had no right.

'Big spiders, like Joy said.'

'Joy?' Why was she looking at me like that? I didn't do anything. 'What's this about spiders?'

'I think a spider bit him. You can see the red spots on his face.'

'Is that what you told him?' She was rocking him like he was a little baby. Bet she never rocked me like that.

'Course I didn't tell him that,' I said shortly. 'I'm not stupid.'

'So what does he mean by big spiders.'

'He's talking 'bout Anancy. He wanted me to read him a story but we don't have any baby books so I told him a 'Nancy story instead.'

'I see.' I didn't like the way she said that. 'Which story did you tell him?'

'Anancy and Brer Bull. Why?'

'Joy, that's so violent. It's no wonder he had night-mares. Couldn't you have found something a bit more appropriate for a three-year-old?' She peered into his face and touched the spots gently. Daniel tried to scratch them but she held his hand away.

'I don't think it's violent,' I said sullenly. 'It just have a lot of action. Children in Jamaica love that story. Anyway I don't think is the story that give him nightmares. I think is that spider that bite him.'

'What spider?' Sophie looked really puzzled and I thought she must be blind.

'Don't you see the red marks on his face?' You wouldn't think she was the one who'd trained as a nurse.

She looked at Daniel and laughed. I couldn't believe she was taking it so lightly. The child could be dying for all she knew.

'For goodness' sake, Joy.' She laughed again. 'That's not a spider bite, he's just got chickenpox.'

Chapter Twenty-Five

We had a few coconuts left over from our trip to Brixton Market. I saw them sitting there in the vegetable rack and suddenly got a craving for coconut drops.

'Sophie, you want the coconut them for anything special?'

'No, did you want to do something with them?'

I shrugged. 'Well, if you not using them, I could make some drops.'

'Go ahead.' And she went back to reading the papers in front of her, on the kitchen table.

I got a bit carried away and as well as the drops I made gizadas. Of course, there were too many for us to eat, especially as Sophie, though she managed to eat a whole gizada, just nibbled at the edge of one of the drops.

'These are good, Joy,' she said.

I snorted. 'That why you eating it like you think it going to turn into a snake or something?'

She smiled. 'Nothing gets past you, does it? These coconut tarts are kind of special but the drops have just a bit too much sugar for me. I've lost my sweet tooth since I left Jamaica.'

That's not the only thing you lost, I thought. 'Coconut tarts!' Why she couldn't say 'gizada' like everybody else?

On Monday morning I was getting an apple from the fruit basket for break when I noticed the plateful of drops and gizadas on the worktop. I lifted the cling film covering them and took one of each. If I had one for lunch every day, I could finish them in a couple weeks. Then I had an idea. I wrapped the whole lot in foil, put them in a carrier bag and left for school.

'What's that?' Alan looked suspiciously at the gizada I held out to him at break.

'Try it an' see.'

He took it and sniffed at it. 'What d'you do with it?'

'Wear it! What you think? Try the thing, you too coward.'

'I'm not a coward!' He took a tiny bite that would have got lost between an ant's teeth and chewed. Then he took another, bigger bite. 'They're not bad. What are they?'

'Gizada. Now try a coconut drops.' I held out the foil.

This time he didn't hesitate, but after the first bite he shook his head. 'I prefer the gizzards. Can I have another? Hey, Mel,' he shouted to Melanie who was just crossing the playground. 'Come try Joy's gizzards!'

'I don't have any gizzard, Alan McKay! I not a fowl. This is gizada.'

161

'Sorry,' he mumbled through a mouthful. 'Here, Mel, try one of these. Give her a gizada, Joy.'

But Melanie looked at the foil and squealed. 'Coconut drops! Can I have one?'

We gaped at her. 'How you know 'bout drops?' I asked.

'My friend in London used to give them to me. Can I?' She took one and bit into it. 'Mmm. Just the way I like them. Lots of ginger.'

'So you know gizada as well?'

She shook her head. 'What are they?'

'Better than drops,' said Alan. 'Try one.'

Alan stopped chewing as we waited for the verdict. Melanie swallowed the first mouthful and frowned. Then she took another bite. The frown grew deeper as she slowly put the rest into her mouth. My heart sank. Well, at least she liked the drops.

'Well?' Alan asked.

'I don't know.' The frown got deeper still. 'I need to try another one to make sure.'

'Oh, you . . .'

Melanie giggled and ducked to avoid Alan's swipe. 'They're really good, Joy,' she said. 'Where did you buy them?'

'I made them.'

'You never!' Alan said.

'You didn't make the pastry for the gizadas though, did you?' Melanie asked.

'That was the easy part. The hardest bit was grating all that coconut.'

'Joy, you're a genius. You could make your fortune selling these.'

I hissed my teeth. 'Melanie, who would want to buy drops and gizada in this place?'

She turned to Alan. 'Would you buy these?'

He dug his hand into his pocket. 'How much?'

'Yeah, right.' I had to laugh. 'I would make a bundle with two customers.'

Melanie took the foil with the rest of the snacks and trotted over to a group of girls who were talking near the fence. From there she went to interrupt the game of football across the playground. She was so much like Nadine. The thought of Nadine filled me with homesickness. I wondered what she was doing.

'Don't look so sad. No one's spat any out yet.'

'Doesn't matter if they did. I only bring them to share with you and Melanie,' I said.

'Right, that's it.' Melanie waved the empty foil when she returned. 'Most of the kids said they would pay a pound, but I think if you charge fifty pence you'd sell more.'

'Melanie, you mad?' I couldn't charge that much for one little drops! It wouldn't feel right.'

'You will never be a millionaire,' Alan sighed.

'I don't want to be a millionaire.' I just wanted enough money to get back to Gran. I stared hard at Melanie and Alan. 'You really think people would buy them?'

Chapter Twenty-Six

I was sitting at the kitchen table pretending to do my homework but, to be honest, I was trying to work out how much money I'd make if I sold thirty gizadas at fifty pence each. If I could sell enough, I'd be back in Jamaica in no time.

'Joy, which of these do you think I should do?'

I looked up to see Sophie holding a pack of spaghetti in one hand and a pack of vermicelli in the other. What was it with her and pasta?

'Why you don't do rice an' peas for a change? You cook pasta two days a' ready this week.'

'I know, but Daniel likes pasta. I'm not sure he'd like rice an' peas.'

'Daniel?'

'Yes, they're coming over tonight, remember?'

'I didn't know that.'

'I told you this morning when you were leaving.' Sophie sighed. So that's what she'd been shouting as I was going through the door. I hadn't bothered to ask her to repeat it 'cause I'd been in a hurry.

'On the other hand,' Sophie continued, Aunt Aimee

164

would enjoy the rice an' peas and Gareth will eat any-thing, so perhaps we should go for that.

'She coming as well?'

'You shouldn't talk about your aunt like that.'

'She's not my aunt actually. She was only married to my grand-uncle, remember?'

'Joy, why are you so . . . oh, I don't have time for this.' She turned to put the pasta on the worktop, then stood massaging her temples. She had deep circles under her eyes and looked tired and washed out.

I couldn't help it. Just for a minute, I felt sorry for her. 'You want me to help you cook the dinner?'

She straightened, looking hopeful. 'Would you mind? I've got a bit of a headache.'

'You go and lie down,' I said, heading for the cup-board. I hadn't forgiven her or anything, and I still didn't trust her, but since I had nothing else I wanted to do and since I didn't fancy pasta again, I thought I might as well. I like cooking anyway.

I couldn't let you do it by yourself,' she protested.

'I cook the dinner for me and Granny every Sunday and I will soon be doing it again. I can manage.'

'Nevertheless, it wouldn't be fair.'

I stifled a snort. *Nevertheless*, I mimicked her accent in my head. She was so English! 'Suit yourself,' I said.

She seasoned the chicken while I did the rice an' peas. There was only one Scotch bonnet pepper left from the batch we'd bought in Brixton at

Christmas. I wondered whether I should cut it up for the chicken or put it whole into the rice. In the end I figured rice an' peas wouldn't be right without the special flavour of the pepper, so I popped it in with the rest of the seasoning, taking care not to break the skin. I didn't want the heat.

Sophie went to the bathroom to take an aspirin for her headache. When she came back I was grating a coconut for the rice an' peas.

'Joy, there's creamed coconut in the fridge. You don't need to do that.'

'Thanks a lot. Now you tell me, when me nearly finish.'

'I'm sorry, I . . .'

'I only joking!'

'Oh.' A small smile tickled the corners of her mouth and I realized I hadn't seen her smile once in the past week. I felt a little twinge of guilt and heard Granny's voice in my head. Except I knew now she wasn't really my gran. And I knew who to thank for that knowledge. The guilt passed.

When the doorbell went, I thought it was Gareth and Daniel, but Mama was standing there when I opened the door. I had to try harder to stop thinking of her as Mama. But it was hard to stop doing something you've been doing all your life, just like that.

'Hi, Joy.'

'Evening, Miss Aimee.'

She looked as if I'd kicked her. She was about to

say something, but when she saw the set look on my face, she changed her mind. 'Where's Sophie?'

'In the kitchen, ma'am.'

She went towards the kitchen and I went into the living room and turned on the television. I didn't move until Gareth and Daniel arrived.

'Hello, Joy,' Gareth said, his eyes searching my face. I don't know what he expected to find, but if it was a smile or a welcome, he was disappointed.

'Hello, Joy.' Daniel copied his dad in his high' lilting voice, and he had such a wide grin on his face that I had to smile then. He looked so funny with his face still spotted from his chickenpox. I was just turning to take them to the dining room when Sophie appeared.

'Gareth, you're here!'

Yes, Einstein, I thought. He kissed her. Right there in front of me. On the lips! I got a strange feeling in the bottom of my stomach. I watched them after that, while we were sitting in the living room having drinks. He kept touching her every chance he got. He pretended to be brushing stuff off, a speck of flour off her cheek, a piece of coconut from her arm, but I knew what he was up to. He just couldn't seem to leave her alone, and she just let him. It was enough to make you sick. And Mama was too involved with Daniel to notice.

'Should I serve up the food now?' I asked, when I couldn't stand it any longer.

Sophie dragged her eyes away from him and looked at me as if surprised to find me there.

'Oh – OK! Thank you, Joy.' She managed to untangle herself from under his arm and stood up. I was going to tell her I could manage on my own, but decided not to. Leave him to himself for a while, I thought. Give his hands a rest.

Sophie was putting the salad on the table and I was putting the rice an' peas in a bowl when Gareth came into the kitchen. Can't he leave her alone for a minute? I wondered. But he'd just come in with the empty glasses.

'Aimee and Daniel are in a world of their own, so I thought I'd come and do some washing up,' he said. 'I'll try not to get in your way.'

I didn't answer.

I was lifting the bowl of rice an' peas when my eyes landed on the Scotch bonnet still in the pan. On impulse, I scooped it up and tucked it inside the rice.

I served Daniel, Mama and Sophie before I reached for Gareth's plate.

'Can I help you to some rice an' peas, Mr Gareth?'

'Thank you, Joy.' His smile was almost as wide as mine. 'This looks delicious, Sophie.'

'You can thank Joy,' Sophie said, smiling at me. She's the cook around here.'

'That's not strictly true.' Give the devil his due, as Gran used to say. 'You not so bad youself when you try.'

Gareth joined in the laughter and then suddenly looked like a lobster who'd jumped into boiling water by mistake. He choked and grabbed at the glass of

168

water beside his plate. He finished that, poured himself another glassful and finished that in one gulp, almost. He'd obviously bitten into the flaming hot Scotch bonnet, first bite.

'Oh, dear, are you all right?' Sophie reached over to pat his back. He looked up, his eyes watering. And caught my eye. I lowered mine, but not fast enough. I could tell he was putting two and two together and getting a perfect four.

'I'm fine,' he said hoarsely. 'A bit just went the wrong way, that's all.'

I looked up, startled. He was looking straight at me. He shot a worried look at Daniel and I scowled. What did he take me for?

'You, OK, Daniel?' I asked.

He nodded. 'I like this chicken,' he mumbled, his mouth full.

When I looked at Gareth again, a small smile was lifting the corners of his mouth. He looked suspiciously at his plate and poured himself another glass of water. He didn't mention the pepper and, though I wasn't joining his fan club or anything, I thought that was very nice of him. He didn't eat very much after that though and neither did I. My appetite had gone on holiday. I'd expected to enjoy Gareth's discomfort, but I just felt flat. I hadn't meant to spoil the whole meal for him and, by the looks of it, for Sophie as well, who naturally noticed that he wasn't eating. She was probably wishing she had gone ahead and cooked the pasta. What was worse, I kept seeing

Gran's face looking at me and it was full of disappointment.

'Maybe you should have some sugar, Gareth,' Mama said, watching him sip at his water.

I nearly jumped out of my seat. He didn't know of course. If he hadn't known not to eat a Scotch bonnet whole, he wouldn't know that sugar would soothe the burning. But Mama would.

'Sugar?' He was puzzled. 'Why?'

'It might bring back you appetite.' She stared at me as she said it. I felt smaller than a flea's baby.

'No thanks, I'm fine. Just not dreadfully hungry. Sorry, Joy, it's no reflection on your food.'

Gareth and Daniel had barely closed the door behind them when Mama laid into me. 'You did it on purpose, didn't you?'

'Did what?' I should have known better than to pretend I didn't know what she was talking about.

'Don't you dare play the dumb innocent with me, girl. You think I don't have eyes in me head?'

I folded my lips and my arms. You don't have no right to lecture me, I thought. You not me mother. But I didn't say anything. Not in the mood she was in.

'What's going on?' Sophie asked. 'What did she do?'

'She only put a whole pepper into Gareth food, nearly kill him.'

'What? Joy, you didn't!'

170

'I didn't know him would be stupid enough to eat it. Everybody know how hot Scotch bonnet pepper is.'

Mama was livid. 'I really losing patience with you now, girl.'

Well you don't have no rights over me, I thought. But my knees were getting a bit weak and my bravado was slinking off to hide in a corner somewhere.

'Oh, Joy, how could you?' Sophie asked sadly. 'That's why he wouldn't eat anything.'

'It was only a little pepper,' I said defensively.

'Only a little pepper!' Mama looked ready to burst. 'The poor man tongue must be swell up by now.'

That's the thing I've noticed about liars. They always like to exaggerate. I wished she would stop it. It was only meant to be a joke. I hadn't expected him to eat the whole thing. And I hadn't expected to feel so bad. And Mama *was* exaggerating. His tongue wouldn't swell up, would it?

Sophie saw my face and took Mama's arm, leading her out of the room. 'It's OK, Aimee,' she said. 'It's my problem, I'll deal with it.'

But her way of dealing with it was to keep out of my way. As soon as Mama left, she went to her room and closed the door, which was fine by me. Until I heard the crying. I hate it when people cry. It always makes me feel funny inside.

Chapter Twenty-Seven

I was cold. I stopped and wrapped the scarf more firmly round my neck. My fingers were like wooden pegs, stiff, clumsy and frozen even in the blue woollen gloves. I know I'm always talking about how cold I am, but I wasn't just whinging. Today I was seriously cold. Whinging. That's a word I learned yesterday and you'll never guess who from. None other than Miss high and mighty Alice Simmonds.

I'd been talking to Alan at break. It had been almost as cold as today. I'd been rubbing my hands together and stamping my feet to keep warm and I hadn't even noticed Alice and her shadow, Karen, skulking behind us. Skulking is another word I picked up. It's one of Mrs Dean's favourite words, I think. After break and lunch she's always telling kids to stop skulking near the door and come into the classroom.

Anyway, I said to Alan, 'Does it ever get warm in this place?'

'Oh, stop whinging,' Miss Nosy butted in. 'If you don't like it here, why don't you go back to your African sunshine? Nobody's keeping you here.'

'Whinging? What does whinging mean?' I asked, like an idiot.

Alice gave an incredulous cackle, which her shadow dutifully copied. 'Don't they teach you anything in Africa?'

I lost my temper then. 'Why you don't just get lost, Alice Simmonds. If you don't have nothing better to do, go and find out where Africa is, since you so interested in the place. Nobody invite you into this conversation. You too eggsup.'

It was her turn to look puzzled. Her copper eyebrows kissed in the middle of her forehead. She turned to Karen, decided she wouldn't get any help there, and turned to Alan instead.

'What's eggs up?' she asked.

'She doesn't know what eggsup means!' I mimicked her disbelieving laughter. 'Don't they teach you anything in England?'

'Good one, Joy,' Alan grinned. Alice looked at him as if he'd hit her, then flounced off, Karen trailing behind. As soon as they were gone, Alan turned to me.

'What *does* eggsup mean?'

'Nosy and interfering,' I told him. 'But don't you dare tell Alice.'

Although I'd been complaining of the cold then, it was like an August heatwave compared to today. Today was *cold*. Icy. Freezing. Arctic. Numbingly cold. Even the penguins would be complaining today. I was bent double by the time I got to school and I felt

173

as though I would never straighten out again. My nose and ears felt like they'd been in the freezer for a week and, even in the thick tights and grey school trousers, my legs felt like the blood had frozen in them. Mrs Dean had to put the lights on in the classroom and, from the huge black frown on the face of the sky, I was sure a storm was on the way. Only I didn't know then what kind of storm.

Just before lunch, while we were doing maths, Mrs Dean raised her head from her marking. 'Oh look, everyone!' she cried. 'It's snowing!'

I'd just finished measuring my last angle and was taking my purse from my bag, getting ready for lunch. It was getting heavy, even though I'd stopped at the newspaper shop on the way to school yesterday and changed most of the coins for notes.

I forgot everything now and dashed with the rest of the class to crowd round the window. Every day since I'd arrived in England I'd been praying for snow and now here it was!

'Pretty, isn't it?' a voice said next to me.

I turned round and grinned at Melanie. 'Pretty? This is heaven!'

'All right, steady on' Mrs Dean laughed. 'No need for the stampede. Looks like it's going to settle, so it will still be there at lunch. Come on, back to your seats.'

I barely heard her. My eyes were stretched to twice their normal size and my mouth rounded in a permanent 'Oh!'

It was as if the angels were having a pillow fight in heaven and the pillows had burst to send all these soft, white feathers floating down to earth. I couldn't wait to get out in it. I wanted to feel it on my face, taste it, smell it. It was so silent. Not like rain or hail. Not like anything. It was as if the world was holding its breath at the beauty of it.

I didn't hear Mrs Dean until she'd called to me twice. I turned round to find the rest of the class waiting for me. The bell had gone and they'd put their books away and were impatient to get out into the snow. I dragged myself away and went back to my table.

'Miss, I can't find my lunch money!' There was a groan from the rest of the class. Sarah Conway lost something at least once a week. Her timing was perfect. She only ever discovered she'd lost it when we were going out to break or lunch and then the whole class had to stay behind until she'd found it. Usually it was in her drawer under all the rubbish she kept in there, or under her chair. I'd never met anyone so forgetful and disorganized.

I opened my bag to take out my purse and my heart gave a flutter of alarm. I scrabbled frantically around the bottom of the bag. Nothing except my history book and my homework diary. I tipped the bag on to the table in front of me and shook out the two books. The flutter in my heart had turned into the pounding of wild horses' hooves by now.

'Have you lost something as well, Joy?' Mrs Dean

175

was on her way to Sarah's table, but she stopped beside me.

'I can't find my purse, Miss.' My voice came out small and choked.

'OK, everybody,' Mrs Dean said briskly. 'Joy and Sarah have lost their money and we can't go to lunch till we find it. So I want you all to look through your things to make sure you haven't got more money than you should have.'

'Miss, there's a purse by the window!' David shouted.

Mrs Dean walked over, picked it up and opened it. Her eyes widened and she came to stand by my table. 'Is this yours, Joy?'

She was holding out my precious purse. My purse with my life savings, my future in it. She knew very well it was mine. I'd written inside on a piece of paper:

Steal not this purse my honest friend, for fear the gallows be your end, or when you die, your soul shall fly, straight down to hell in a coconut shell.

I'd stuck that on the top flap. On the bottom I'd pasted another piece of paper on which I'd written:

If this purse should chance to roam, just box its ears and send it home to Joy Patterson, 21A Oakridge Avenue.

That's as much as I could get on it, but I figured most people would know where Oakridge Avenue was, so they didn't need the rest of the address anyway.

I must have dropped it on the way to the window. I felt a bit foolish for panicking like that, but I knew my life would be over if I lost it. I went to take it from Mrs Dean, but she carefully closed it and kept hold of it.

'There's rather a lot of money here, Joy,' she said.

'Yes, Miss.' I knew there was a lot of money there. It was mine, wasn't it? She didn't need to tell me that.

'Where did you get all this?' She weighed the purse in her hand, her eyes keen on my face.

'My mother gave it to me, Miss.' It was weird talking about Sophie as my mother.

Mrs Dean's eyes narrowed. 'You know you're not allowed to bring large sums like this to school, don't you?' I didn't as a matter of fact, but I supposed it made sense. Look what nearly happened.

'Is there a reason you had all this on you today?'

'I didn't want to leave it at home in case we got burgled,' I said. A ripple of laughter started at Alice's table and ran round the classroom. I didn't care. I couldn't very well tell them I carried my money around with me because I didn't want Sophie to find it.

Mrs Dean was frowning. 'It's not safe to carry so much around with you. You'd better take it to the office for safe keeping until home time. You should consider putting it in a bank until you're ready to use it. She weighed it in her hand again and a smile played around her lips. You'd earn interest on it as well as making sure burglars couldn't get at it.'

What a good idea. How much interest could I earn in a month? I wished Nadine was here, or that I'd concentrated harder when we were doing simple interest in Prospect.

'Miss, what about *my* money,' Sarah wailed.

'Oh, yes. How much have you lost, Sarah?'

The search continued but there was no sign of a stray five-pound note anywhere. Everyone else had a few coins. Nobody had any notes. Nobody, that is, except me. Alice was the one to say it, naturally, but I knew everyone was thinking it.

'Mrs Dean, perhaps Joyanna took Sarah's money.' She paused to let her words sink in, but not long enough for Mrs Dean to tell her off, before adding, 'By mistake.'

Mrs Dean sighed. 'Joy, do you know how much money you had in here?'

I told her.

There were gasps from several tables.

She frowned. 'That *is* rather a lot of money. Do you mind if we count it, just to make sure you haven't picked up Sarah's by mistake?'

I shook my head.

It was all there, of course. Just as I'd said. I'd counted it that morning before I left the flat, so I should know.

Mrs Dean gave another weary sigh. 'All right, everyone, you may go to lunch now. Sarah, go to the

178

office and ask them to give you a lunch voucher for today. We'll try and sort this out after lunch. Joy, I'll take this to the office for safe keeping. You can collect it at home time.'

The snow was settling by the time we got into the playground. I raced around with the rest of the school, but while most of them were making snowballs and chucking them at each other, I was trying to catch the flakes in my hands and on my tongue. I was surprised at how difficult it was to catch them. They just seemed to float gently, but mockingly, out of reach. By the time the bell went, we were all hot and tired. Surprisingly, now that the snow was falling, it wasn't that cold any more.

As we filed into the classroom, Mrs Dean took my arm and held me back, letting the others pass. 'OK, Six D, take out your reading books for silent reading.' She guided me through the door and half-closed it, leaving it open just enough so she could keep an eye on the class without them hearing what she was saying.

'Joy.' She looked troubled and I wondered what catastrophe had happened now. 'We tried calling your mother.' I raised startled eyes to her face. Had something happened to Sophie? 'We wanted to remind her not to send so much money into school with you in future.'

'But she doesn't know about the money,' I said, alarmed.

Now she was perplexed. But you told me your mother gave you that money. Which is it?'

179

'Both, Miss.' I hurried on because I could see she was losing patience. 'It's my lunch money and pocket money I've been saving up for – for something special.'

'I see. Joy, are you sure you didn't take Sarah's money . . . ?' She stopped and pushed the door open. Alice's slave was standing by the door and I could see she had been listening. Her stuck-out ears were almost vibrating. I wished I knew how long she'd been there.

'Karen, what are you doing out of your seat?' Mrs Dean was livid. Karen held up a pencil and sharpener for us to see.

'Sharpening my pencil, Miss.'

'Why do you need a pencil for silent reading? Get back to your table this minute.'

But the damage was done. By the time we got back into the classroom I could tell by the way they were all looking at me that I was officially a liar and a thief.

Chapter Twenty-Eight

The headmaster's secretary came to the classroom before the bell went for the end of school. She spoke in an undertone to Mrs Dean, gave her an envelope and then went out. Mrs Dean called me back as I was going through the door.

She shooed out the four children who were dawdling, I expect to find out what more trouble I could possibly have got in to.

'I've got a letter here for your mum,' she said, once we were alone. 'The headmaster has decided it's best – safest – if we keep the money here until your mum comes in. He doesn't think you should be walking the streets with all that cash on you.' Her gaze was sympathetic but I wasn't fooled. What she really meant was that Mr Murray thought I'd stolen it. I'm not stupid. If Sophie didn't know anything about it, and I said she'd given it to me, what was he to think, especially as there was still no sign of Sarah's money?

I dawdled on the way home. It had stopped snowing and there was a thin white sheet on the roofs and in the fields, but on the road and pavements, it had turned to an ugly brown slush. It looked like the shaved ice we bought in paper cones back home except that, instead of being sprayed with sweet red or yellow syrup, this had been sprayed with mud. Even so, I liked the soft squishy sound it made under my boots and I purposely walked on every bit of slush I could see.

Call me a coward, but I couldn't face an interrogation from Sophie. When I got home, I put my bag in my room and didn't say a word about the letter. I waited until she was going through the door next morning.

'Oh, I got a letter from school for you yesterday,' I said, as if I'd only just remembered and I hadn't been worrying about it all night.

'Have you? Where is it?'

'In my bag, I'll get it.' I took as long as I could till Sophie shouted at me.

'Hurry up, Joy. I'm going to be late.'

She turned the letter over, frowning. 'Why didn't you give this to me yesterday? It might be important.'

I opened my mouth to say 'I forgot', but Gran's voice was there in my head: 'Lying lips are an abomination to the Lord.' I shrugged and kept silent.

'Well I haven't got time to read it now.' Sophie stuffed the letter into the side pocket of her handbag. 'I'll read it later.'

Melanie and Alan were waiting for me at the school gates. Alan grinned at my surprised expression as they fell into step beside me. 'We thought you could do with some moral support after yesterday.'

'Thanks.'

Melanie peered up at me. 'Are you all right?'

I nodded. 'Better now.' It was such a relief to know they didn't believe I was a thief.

The bell went and we started walking to the lines together.

'Alan, I wouldn't talk to her if I were you. People might think you're a thief as well.'

'Don't answer that, Alan,' I said as he opened his mouth to reply. 'It's not worth it.'

But Melanie wasn't letting that go. 'Alice,' she said sweetly. 'Do you know what slander is?'

'And do you know what the penalty for slander is?' Alan joined in. 'Two years in prison wasn't it, Melanie?'

'Five years, last I heard,' Melanie replied.

Alice threw us all a poisonous look and flounced off to join Karen at the head of the line.

I turned to Alan. 'Is that true?'

He shrugged. 'Ask Melanie.'

'Melanie?'

She gazed calmly at me. 'I've no idea,' she said.

I waited all day for the summons to the office, but when it came I was totally unprepared. We were in the middle of an art lesson, about two-thirty, and I was absorbed in painting the leaves of my star-apple tree a rich, deep copper. I didn't hear Mrs Dean call me and Carol, who was sitting opposite, had to nudge me before I realized.

'Come in, Joyanna.' Mr Murray smiled. Sophie

was sitting in one of the leather chairs in front of his desk and he motioned me to the other.

'Hello, Joy.' I'd never seen Sophie looking as serious.

'Hi.' That's all I could manage under Mr Murray's eagle gaze.

Mr Murray leaned forwards, elbows on his desk. He made a steeple of his fingers and considered them for a while, as if he was searching for the right words to begin.

'Thank you for coming in, Miss Patterson,' he began at last. 'It appears Joy's come in to school with rather a large sum of money. As you know, we don't encourage children to carry too much cash around. But I understand you don't know anything about this?'

Sophie shook her head, her eyes fastened on my face.

'Ah. I see.'

'It's my money,' I said hotly. I knew what he was thinking.

'We'd just like to establish where you got it from.'

I glanced at Sophie. Her face could've been carved out of granite and I couldn't tell what she was thinking.

'She gave it to me,' I mumbled.

Mr Murray sighed. 'But, Joyanna, your mother has no knowledge of the seventy pounds.'

'Seventy pounds!' Sophie burst out. They'd obviously not told her how much it was. 'Where did you get it?'

'You gave it to me.'

'Don't lie to me, Joy.'

That hurt. I will admit I can be a chatterbox, sometimes insensitive. I can be selfish, even, now and then, impulsive. But I was not a liar. I glared at her. 'I'm not lying. You gave it to me – well, most of it – for lunch and pocket money. The rest I got from selling gizadas.'

Sophie looked horrified and Mr Murray's eyebrows jumped up to say hello to his bald patch.

'You were *selling* those gizadas? I thought you were making them to give to your friends.'

'I needed the money.'

'What for? Joy, are you in some kind of trouble?'

There was no point in keeping it a secret any longer. 'I was saving up for my fare back to Jamaica,' I said. Sophie made a sound as if someone was trying to strangle her.

There was a knock on the door and Mrs Dean pushed her head through the door.

'I thought you might like to know that Sarah's just told me she found her five pounds,' she said. 'She'd left it at home.'

Mr Murray glanced at her. 'Thank you, Mrs Dean.' I was in the clear at last, but too late for me to enjoy it. At the moment I was taking in Sophie's expression. She looked at me as if she'd never seen me before.

'You really want to go back to Jamaica!'

I rolled my eyes heavenwards. Wasn't that what I'd been telling her for weeks? But, like a typical adult, she hadn't bothered to listen because what I wanted wasn't important. It hadn't been important when I was a baby and it wasn't now. I was feeling angry and fed up. If I hadn't been, I wouldn't have said what I ended up saying to Sophie.

Chapter Twenty-Nine

We walked out of Mr Murray's office in silence. I tried to judge whether Sophie was raging angry or extremely upset, but her face was a rigid mask. I couldn't read anything from it.

'I'm going to the classroom to get my bag,' I said when we were in the corridor. Sophie carried on as if she hadn't heard. Luckily the classroom was empty when I got there. I couldn't face anyone just now and I couldn't deal with the nosy stares of Six D. I grabbed my bag and dashed out. I was anxious to explain to Sophie that I hadn't meant to say all those things in Mr Murray's office. But when I got back into the corridor, she wasn't there. I rushed to the entrance. She would be waiting on the steps probably. But she wasn't. The yard was deserted. Sophie had gone home without me.

If anyone had been watching me on my way home they'd have thought I was going bonkers. I kept hurrying, almost running, and then slowing to a crawl, almost standing still. I wanted to see Sophie, apologize, tell her I didn't mean it, ask her to forgive me. And I didn't want to see Sophie. Didn't want to

187

see the dead look in her eyes, see her trying hard not to look at me, see the dislike on her face when she did look at me.

I'd been trying to get back at her since I found out she was my mother. The silences, the rudeness, were supposed to make her react. She was always so calm when I was just a boiling pot of anger and confusion. I think I resented her for that.

Until today she'd just pretended there was nothing wrong, calm, no matter how unfriendly and rude I was. Long-suffering, Gran would call it. But today was different. Even without trying, I'd made her angry. Angry enough to leave without me. I should be happy, triumphant. But I just felt sick in my stomach. I'd humiliated her in public.

I went into the kitchen as soon as I got home. That's where Sophie usually was when I got back from school. She would be making the dinner or putting a wash into the machine. But she wasn't there. I left my bag on the kitchen table and hurried to the living room. I'd decided to apologize and I wanted to get it over with before I lost my nerve. I kept seeing her stony face in my mind and the more I saw it the more scared I got. The living room was empty. Her bedroom door was closed. I knocked. Nothing. I pushed it open, cautiously, and stuck my head into the room. She wasn't there either.

There was only one other place she could be. She'd be in my bedroom, collecting my clothes for the wash. She couldn't have gone out because she never left the flat without telling me where she was going. And she was always home when I got in from school. That was the whole reason she went to work so early every morning, so she could leave early to be home when I got back.

I pushed open the door. 'Sophie, I didn't . . .' I stopped. You can look pretty silly talking to an empty room. I slumped on to the bed. My knees were wobbling like jelly on a plate, my hands shaking like a leaf in a hurricane and there was a block of ice the size of Blue Mountain in the space where my heart was supposed to be. I didn't know what to do. That is when I thought to see if her car was gone. It was.

I knew what I'd do. I'd go and prepare the dinner so that she wouldn't have to cook when she came in. She'd be tired from work and having to visit school and everything. If there was a hot meal waiting for her when she came in, it would put her in a better mood. If she came back.

I got up and headed for the door. I felt a little better now that I had something to do. I was nearly at the door when I heard a car coming through the gate. I ran to the window and drew back the curtains, but it was Mama's beaten-up car, not Sophie's shiny red one, which was pulling into the drive.

Mama! Mama would know what to do.

Her eyebrows climbed up her forehead when she saw me waiting by the door. 'Hi, Joy.' She smiled, a slight, wary parting of her lips. Not the crease-up-the-face smile she used to give me before I found out who she was. This smile wasn't expecting an answering one. And it wasn't disappointed. I felt like I would never smile again.

'Where's Sophie?' Mama asked.

'I don't know.' I did try, but I just couldn't stop the tremor in my voice or the trembling of my lips. Any fool could see straight away that something was wrong and Mama was no fool. She frowned.

'What happen, Joy?'

The words tumbled out of my mouth. 'I didn't mean to say it, Mama, honest. It just sort of jump out of me mouth and then Mr Murray said Sophie should think about having counselling and I think that made her really angry and now I don't know where she gone.' It didn't even make sense to me, so I wasn't all that surprised to see the look of confusion on Mama's face.

'Why don't you come upstairs and tell me everything.' I nearly cracked then. Mama didn't have a single reason to be so gentle with me. I'd been pig awful to her and Sophie for weeks, but she was acting like none of that had happened.

When we were sitting on the sofa, I poured out the whole thing to her up to when I'd said I was going back to Jamaica. Then I stopped. Shame was killing me and I couldn't go on.

Mama frowned. 'That shouldn't upset her more than usual. You been saying that since you find out I not you mother.'

'She wasn't upset about that. Least I don't think she was.'

'Oh?'

I closed my eyes and saw Sophie's face again, wide-eyed with the sudden realization that I really wanted to go back to Jamaica. I'd felt hurt and angry that she hadn't taken me seriously until then. I suppose she thought I'd just been saying it to spite her. I don't know why that made me so mad. I guess I was just fed up with feeling confused and guilty and unwanted and not knowing who I was. So when she had said, 'You really want to go back to Jamaica!' in that sort of 'I can't believe it' voice, like I'd hit her or something – well, I couldn't handle the feelings inside me any more.

'Well, what did you expect?' I had yelled. 'You can't just bring me over here to tell me you me mother and then expect me to jump for joy.'

Mr Murray had inhaled loudly and Sophie had gasped.

'Joy!'

I should have stopped then, but I didn't.

'First you don't want me, so you give me away. Then when you feel like, you decide you want me after all. Well I not a parcel you can throw down and pick up as you please, and you can't have me, 'cause I going home to Granny. I don't know why you couldn't left things how they stay. You have to go and spoil everything.'

I had clasped my hands tight in my lap. They were

shaking. My heart was pounding, and I stared at the floor without seeing it. There was a sort of film in front of my eyes. The silence stretched painfully on and on.

And then Mr Murray had offered to contact a counsellor for us. I'd never seen Sophie look like that. She glared at him and her voice was menacingly quiet.

'Pardon me?'

Mr Murray had opened his mouth, thought better of it and closed it again sharpish. Sophie had got up, said, 'Excuse me,' in a tight little voice and headed for the door. I didn't know what else to do. I had followed her.

Granny always said, when you're angry you should count to ten silently before you say anything. Mama must've been really angry because it looked like she was silently counting to a million.

'Joy,' she said eventually. I was bracing myself for the tongue-lashing I knew was coming, but she didn't sound angry. Just weary. 'There's something I think you should know about your mother. She tell you already that she was only sixteen when she found out she was going to have you?'

'Sixteen!' That's the same age as Elaine. I couldn't imagine Elaine with a baby.

Mama nodded. 'A child she-self. Well that was when she find out about her own mother. She always thought her mother was dead. Her grandfather was boiling when him find out she was carrying you.

192

That's why him let it out that her mother dumped her with them when she was six months old, gone off to America and nobody hear a thing from her since. Bad blood, him call it. Say you mother inherited her mother's bad blood.'

I sucked in my breath. 'That was so cruel!'

'Mmm.' Mama nodded. 'Him was not an easy man to get on with. He had a position to hold up in the church and I think him was afraid of what people would say. A elder supposed to be able to control him own house after all.'

'Yes, but I mean Sophie's mother too.'

'Don't be too harsh on her. From what I hear, she was only young herself, and Bob, Sophie's father, was still studying, so neither of them could look after a child. But, as you can imagine, poor Sophie was really upset.'

I knew how she felt, except that she must have felt much worse than I did. She didn't even know who her mother was. 'So how could she do the same thing to me?'

'She did not!' Mama said fiercely. 'Her grandfather tell her to leave him house and not to come back unless she give the baby up for adoption. I beg her to let me adopt you, we couldn't have children you see, so you would have been a godsend.' She gave me a wistful smile. 'But Sophie wouldn't hear of it. Say could I just look after you for her until she could look after you herself. She stay with us for a while, then she and me and you da . . . John, we go up to

193

Kingston together. When we come back few months later, I have a baby girl.'

She pushed herself up and headed for the kitchen, white uniform rustling and nurse's shoes squeaking on the carpet. 'I feel I need a cup of tea. You want something to drink?'

When we were sipping our drinks, she her tea and I a cup of Milo, I asked the question I'd been thinking about for a while. There was something I had to know. I was almost too scared to ask. 'Did Gran . . . ?'

Mama shook her head. 'Your gran – great gran – is a good woman. But in her day a woman do what her husband tell her.'

She was silent and I could see she was back in Jamaica, eleven years before. 'I would o' do anything to keep you, but Sophie was determined to look after you herself. She near make herself sick working two, three jobs over the years so she could send you clothes and money, buy this place and send for you.'

I gulped. Sophie had sent the clothes and money?

She read my thoughts in my expression. 'Yes, I know you always thought it was me. A few things were from me, yes, but Sophie is the one who went wild.'

There was the sound of a car coming into the drive and my heart immediately started practising for the Olympic hundred-metre race. I didn't think I could face Sophie now. When I thought how I wouldn't listen when she tried to tell me how it was, how selfish I was, I just wanted to bury my head in a hole.

When I thought how I'd accused her of not caring, in front of Mr Murray, I wanted to die.

Mama stared hard at me. 'I tell you this for one reason. I want you to go easy on Sophie. She been through enough already.' She got up and crossed to the window. 'Well, you mother is here now. You better go on down. She'll be wondering where you is.'

Chapter Thirty

When I opened the door to the living room, they were standing by the French windows.

'Joy! Where have you been?'

What? I didn't get it. Hadn't she missed me? I'd come home scouring the house to find her and she'd forgotten my existence.

'Upstairs with Mama,' I said. Only the slight raising of her brows betrayed her surprise. She knew I hadn't been upstairs for weeks.

I should have said hello to Gareth, but I didn't. I wanted to talk to Sophie really badly, but not in front of an audience, and especially not in front of him. I'd prepared myself for this heart to heart, but I couldn't very well grovel in front of him, could I?

'Does this mean you're not mad at Aunt Aimee any more?'

'Why don't we sit down,' Gareth said, before I could answer.

Why don't you go home and leave us alone? I thought. For a horrible moment I imagined I'd said it aloud, but his glance only lasted a second and neither of them said anything. That was a relief at least.

I sat in the far corner of the room on the edge of the armchair. They sat kneecap to kneecap on the sofa.

'So, I hear you're on your way back to Jamaica, Joy,' Gareth said. 'I'm sorry you don't like it here.'

Just like that. I stared at Sophie. I was expecting her to try to talk me out of going back. I hadn't expected her just to accept it and to tell Gareth about it, like it was all arranged.

'We'll have to let Granny know you're coming back, of course,' Sophie said. 'But you should be back in Jamaica by Easter.'

'I don't know if I'll have enough money by Easter,' I said quietly.

'I think I can manage to buy you a plane ticket.' Sophie laughed.

I frowned at her. She wasn't behaving like Sophie. But then I wasn't behaving like myself either. It was only yesterday I was counting the money and thinking a couple more weeks and I'd have enough. Now, suddenly, the idea of going back didn't seem so appealing. I thought of the big send-off Gran had given me, the long, tearful farewells and the excited letters I'd written that first week, telling them how great England was in spite of the cold. And then I thought of myself arriving back in Jamaica barely a month later and the explanations I'd have to give.

None of this had mattered before, but now they seemed like major obstacles.

And Sophie didn't want me. Mama was wrong. Maybe she had when I'd been a baby, but she didn't now. If she did, she would be begging me to stay with her, not be so anxious to get rid of me.

'And since you find it so difficult to be in my company, we'll see if we can't arrange for you to stay with Aunt Aimee until you leave.'

The mask slipped for a minute and her voice shook. She didn't look at me but I could see the way her lips trembled and her hand curled into a tight fist, as if she was trying hard not to cry. My heart lifted. Maybe *I* was wrong.

'I'm sorry, Sophie. I didn't mean what I said,' I said through the lump in my throat.

'That wasn't a very nice thing to do, was it?' Gareth said.

It was OK to be told off by Sophie. She had a right. But this was none of his business. 'I wasn't talking to you. Do you have to tell him everything?' I scowled at Sophie. Just when I thought we were getting somewhere he had to go and spoil it.

'Joy, don't be so rude!'

How come when I was rude to her she didn't say a word, but now she was angry because I'd asked a perfectly reasonable question? And she was angry. Her eyes were flashing and her nostrils dilating like a mad bull in a pen.

'Well I don't see why he has to know everything

about me. You couldn't be bothered to tell me Mama was not my real mother, but you couldn't wait to tell him. Even Daniel, you could tell him, but not me. The whole world knew about my parents before I did.'

'That was my fault,' Gareth butted in before Sophie could do any more than open her mouth. 'I told Daniel we were buying a present for Sophie's daughter. I didn't realize you hadn't been told. Don't blame your mother.'

'But why did you have to know in the first place? It's nothing to do with you? If I had given my child away, I wouldn't be in a hurry to tell everyone about it.'

I knew I was not being fair, especially after what Mama had told me, but Gareth just seemed to drive every bit of reasonableness out of my head. I couldn't believe I'd actually liked him when I first met him.

'Joy, there's something we have to tell you,' Sophie said. She turned to Gareth as if seeking support and he took her other hand in his.

'You're sure about this now?' His gaze softened on her face. I stared at them, at their clasped hands, as if mesmerized.

'Joy,' Sophie said, and I watched her fingers tighten round Gareth's hand. 'Gareth and I . . . Gareth's asked me to marry him.'

I just sat there, as though I was turned to stone. I didn't know what to say. I knew what I was expected to say, of course. Congratulations. I'm so happy for you. But I wasn't. I felt like I'd just run headlong into Maas Josh's handcart again and all the wind was knocked out of me.

Married! He would be my stepdad. It was bad enough when they were going out together, but married? I knew they liked each other, obviously, but enough to get married? That was serious. My head spun.

'So you see, I had to tell Gareth about you. You do understand, don't you, Joy?'

I didn't reply.

'We were going to wait until you got a bit more used to having me around,' Gareth said. 'But since you're going back to Jamaica, there doesn't seem to be much point in waiting any longer.'

He was looking at me expectantly, as if he wanted me to say something, but I'd barely heard him. There was a huge hole in the pit of my stomach and I think my heart had fallen into it because I couldn't feel it beating. I wanted to run and hide from them, from the ache inside, but I couldn't move. My hands, my feet, my whole body felt heavy and sluggish, as if made of lead.

'We were hoping you'd be bridesmaid,' Sophie said. 'That's why I wanted you to come over from Jamaica so early. We were – we are planning to get married in the summer.'

A picture came into my mind then. A snapshot of Sophie, Gareth and Daniel posing for the camera. One happy family with no room for anyone else.

'That's why you're so anxious to send me back,' I thought aloud. 'You're happy enough with Gareth and Daniel.'

'Joy! That's not true.'

Gareth uncoiled himself from the sofa and got to his feet. 'I'm going to collect Daniel,' he said. He saw the desperate expression on Sophie's face and reached down to squeeze her hand. 'I won't be long, but I think you two need to talk this through alone.'

When he was gone, Sophie came to sit next to me. She took my hand in hers. 'Joy, I want you to answer me truthfully. Do you want to go back to Jamaica?'

I opened my mouth to say of course I did. I didn't want to stay where I wasn't wanted. Then I snapped it shut again. Truthfully, she'd said. Did I want to go back to Jamaica after the fuss everyone had made about my leaving? Did I want to see the disappointment on Gran's face? Because although she would be glad to see me, she would be disappointed as well. Disappointed that I'd failed to make it here. Did I want to leave Sophie with Gareth and Daniel? Definitely not, I thought fiercely. Much as I liked Daniel, I wasn't just going to hand Sophie over to him. She was *my* mother.

I shook my head.

Sophie's hand tightened over mine. She closed her eyes and let out her breath in a huge sigh of relief.

'Thank goodness. I wasn't looking forward to keeping you here against your will.'

'Keeping me . . . ? But you said you were planning to send me back.'

'Not on your life. D'you think I spent the last eleven years trying to have you with me just to send you back?'

'So then why did you say I would be back in Jamaica by Easter?'

'Gareth thought we should call your bluff. He didn't think you really wanted to leave. I'm so glad he was right.' She saw my expression and the smile disappeared. 'Joy, can I ask you a favour?'

'What?'

'Will you give Gareth a chance? He's not that bad, you know.' That's debatable, I thought, but I just shrugged. She smiled, resigned, and squeezed my shoulder. It felt good. I snuggled up to her and smiled at her. She looked startled. Her arm crept round me, shyly at first, as if she wasn't quite sure what my reaction would be. I snuggled closer. We sat like that until the doorbell went.

Sophie got up reluctantly and went to let Gareth in. I wasn't sure I wanted to see him yet, so I slipped through the French windows into the garden. There were little knobs on the tree. Green knobs. Little buds were forming all over the branches. Sophie was right, the tree was going to live again.

I took a step closer and something scrunched under my feet. The ground was covered with little shoots, green shoots peeping out like mice from their holes. Even the sunshine felt warmer and the earth had a rich musty smell that I'd never noticed before. This was a good sign. Winter wouldn't last forever after all. I turned towards the French windows and stopped. Perhaps I would go through the kitchen.

Chapter Thirty-One

We were at the school fair and Melanie was insisting on visiting every stall. Mrs Dean was in charge of the tombola.

'Enjoying it, you two?'

'Yes, thank you, Miss,' Melanie said. I was busy opening a ticket.

'I won! I won!' I waved the ticket above my head, jumping up and down.

'OK, let's have it then.' Mrs Dean laughed. She looked great in her cowboy outfit, I have to say. It was the first time I'd seen her hair loose. It fell in thick dark waves to her shoulder and bounced underneath her cowboy hat when she moved. She was very pretty, Mrs Dean.

I gave her the ticket. Melanie was still struggling to tear hers open without ripping it in two. 'How'd you do this thing?' she asked. Mrs Dean was trying to find my prize among all the toys, sweets and colouring stuff on the shelf behind her. I reached out to take Melanie's ticket and then I stopped.

'Would you like me to see if I can open it?'

She nodded.

I tore off the edge and gave it back to her.

'So that's the way to do it.' She read the words in a resigned voice. '"Sorry, no luck this time. Try again." Yeah, right.'

Mrs Dean handed over a huge box of chocolates. 'There you are, Joy,' she said with a smile. 'Mind you don't eat them all at once.'

I grinned. 'Sorry, Miss, I couldn't do that.'

She looked puzzled. 'Do what?'

'What you just told me to do. Eat them all at once.'

'But I didn't . . .' She stopped. 'Déjà, vu,' she said slowly.

'Yep.' Melanie was staring intently at me. So was Mrs Dean.

'Joy, what exactly did I just say?'

I thought for a second. 'There you are, Joy, mind you don't eat them all at once.' I repeated it word for word.

Mrs Dean nodded. 'And what does that mean?'

'Make sure you eat them all at once.'

She was shaking her head, but she was smiling. '"Mind you don't" means "make sure you don't" in England.'

'And "mind you" means "make sure you do?"' I said slowly.

She nodded.

'Not in Jamaica,' I said. 'It's the other way round, there'

'But in England,' Mrs Dean said.

'So when you said, "mind you collect all the books . . ."'

'Precisely,' said Melanie. I grinned.

Mrs Dean grinned. 'I'm glad that's sorted,' she said.

Melanie stuck a lolly in her mouth. I transferred the box of chocolates into my left hand. It was getting pretty crowded, what with the monkey I'd bought for Daniel and the rag doll I'd won in the raffle. I linked my free hand through Melanie's. 'See you later, Miss,' I said. I was almost skipping as we made our way to the food stall.

'What time's your mum getting here?' Melanie asked as she took the burger from the dad in charge of the burger stand.

'About four, she said.'

She took a bite out of the burger. 'Do you think she'd let you come over and play?'

'I'm sure she will.' I couldn't hide my delight. Then I sobered as a thought occurred to me. 'But are you sure *your* parents won't mind?'

'Positive. Come and meet them.'

'They're here?'

She nodded. 'On the flower stall. My dad's crazy about plants and my mum likes to humour him.'

Mrs Forbes was a replica of Melanie. Or should that be the other way around? Same short blonde hair, same candid grey eyes, even the same round glasses. If Melanie had been twenty years older, they'd have been mistaken for twins, I'm sure. The only difference was that whereas Melanie was usually serious as a judge, Mrs Forbes's face was creased into a smile. I liked her at once.

Mr Forbes was the serious one. He was the surprise. He had to stoop to stop his head banging against the ceiling of the flower tent. Must be painful having to go around bent double like that all day, I thought. But he didn't seem too concerned. As he pushed the unruly red hair out of his eyes, I thought that with his great, bushy beard he looked like a big, shaggy bear. He took my hand and pumped it up and down, peering solemnly at me. 'So this is Joy,' he said. And then with a strong Jamaican accent, 'Wha' happen, Joy?'

They all three laughed at my astonishment. 'We used to live in Brixton,' Melanie explained. 'We have a lot of Jamaican friends there and we go up to see them every now and then.'

So that's how come she was so sure my accent was Jamaican. 'You might have warned me,' I said.

'And missed that look on your face?'

Melanie was right. They were really pleased that she wanted me to come over. 'A capital idea,' said Mr Forbes, and went off to serve a customer.

'Why don't you come over for your tea after the fair?' Mrs Forbes suggested. It would be great, of course, but I was a bit dubious.

'I'd have to ask my mum,' I told her. 'She'll be here,' I glanced at my watch, 'in about half an hour.'

'Well, bring her over when she comes. We'd love to meet her.'

'Fancy a go on the coconut shy?' asked Melanie.

We were nearly there, when I stopped. 'Oh-oh.' I tugged at Melanie's arm. 'Let's try the coconut shy later.'

She followed my glance to where Alice and Karen were standing, next to the stall, licking ice creams and watching the stunt bikes. 'Joy, you really shouldn't let them . . .'

'It's all right for you,' I interrupted. 'You haven't been . . .' I stopped, rephrased it. 'Have you ever been picked on because people don't like the way you look?'

'Yep.'

I looked at her closely. 'Alice?'

'Yep.'

I was intrigued. Alice didn't seem to bother with Melanie these days. Not unless Melanie was with me, and then her snide remarks were only half-hearted. I was dying to know how Melanie had managed that. 'What happened?'

'Well, I couldn't talk to Mum and Dad about it. It would hurt them as well.'

'So?'

Melanie hesitated as if she wasn't sure how I'd take the next bit. 'I talked to someone from church.'

'You go to church?'

'Sure. Why are you looking so surprised?'

'Nothing. Is just – I can come with you on Sunday?'

'Nope.'

'Oh.'

'I go to church on Saturday.'

'Oh.'

Melanie laughed. 'You're welcome to come with me any Sabbath you like. Anyway, as I was saying, I talked to my Sabbath school teacher and she reminded me that "a soft answer turns away wrath, but a harsh word stirs up anger."'

'Hey, I used to have to recite that in Sunday school!'

'Well, try using it.'

I looked at her with my eyebrows raised, disbelieving.

'People can't keep being nasty to you if you don't seem bothered.'

I wasn't convinced, but I was willing to try anything.

I watched with a sense of doom as Alice turned, stared at us and nudged Karen. They strolled towards us and I immediately thought of hyenas closing in on a baby deer.

'Look who's here!' Alice drawled. Her tongue flicked out over the ice cream. A snake, I thought. A sly serpent is what she reminds me of. 'If it isn't four-eyes and the giraffe.'

'Lovely to see you too, Alice.' I couldn't believe Melanie could be so calm. I could feel the flame of anger flickering inside already. Melanie must've sensed the tension in me because she linked her arm though mine and, Alice couldn't see it, but I felt the slight pressure of her hand encouraging me to keep calm.

'Yes, it's nice to see you, Alice.' I forced myself to

smile. 'I like that top you have on, it look nice on you.' I hate to admit it, but the green top did look good on her. At least I didn't have to lie as well as crawl. If this didn't work I was going to strangle Melanie.

Alice frowned, not sure if I was making fun of her, but Melanie joined in.

'Yeah, green suits you,' she said.

'Um, thanks,' Alice said warily.

'Well, see you, Alice.' Melanie grabbed my arm and marched off.

'Bye, Alice.'

'Bye,' she said in a bemused voice.

'Why you do that, Melanie? I was just starting to enjoy meself.'

'Yeah, and she nearly got suspicious. I only meant you to say hi to her, not go overboard like that.' She stopped and mimicked my voice. 'I like that top you have on.'

'I don't talk like that. And anyway, it worked, didn't it?' I giggled. 'Did you see her face?'

Melanie nodded. 'That was so funny!'

I thought I heard Gran's disapproving voice, but it was very faint so I couldn't be sure. Right now I was enjoying my only complete triumph over Alice. I'd repent later.

A hand touched me on the shoulder and I spun round. 'Sophie!'

'Having a good time?' she asked, smiling.

'It's great!' I said. I saw Melanie looking at her

expectantly. 'Oh, Melanie, meet my mum.' I hesitated, but only slightly. 'Mum, this is my friend Melanie.'

The look on my mum's face was worth a million pounds.

ELLEN POTTER

OLIVIA KIDNEY

Enter the weird and wonderful world of Olivia Kidney. She's about to discover that there's no place as crazy as home!

Olivia can't find the keys to her new apartment block. Neither can she find her dad, the caretaker. Where is he? As her search takes her from floor to floor, Olivia discovers that this is one strange place to live. Here, it's perfectly normal to come across a bunch of multi-coloured talking lizards, wall-to-wall tropical rainforest, and a family that keeps a goat in their living room! Just what is going on? And will opening these doors allow Olivia to face the mysteries of her own life . . . ?

Martine Murray

The slightly true story of
Cedar B. Hartley
(who planned to live an unusual life)

Meet Cedar B. Hartley. She's exasperating. She's potentially infamous. And her life is about to be overturned . . .

There's no one quite like Cedar. She's got hellish red hair, a super-shaggy dog called Stinky, and she'd love to be a brilliant gymnast. She's also very sad that her funny, crazy brother, Barnaby, has run away.

Kite's arrival turns Cedar's life upside down in every way. Mysterious and with a voice like a river, he amazes her with his incredible acrobatic skills. Together they're going to put on the greatest show ever (featuring fearless moves such as the helicopter and the bluebird). But as Kite teaches Cedar how to fly, he also helps her to discover someone new and powerful within herself – someone who is finally ready to face her family's secrets and her own special place in the world.

A deliciously quirky first novel with an irresistible heroine (and an even better dog).